She wore only a chemise. A wet chemise

Simon's breath halted, and for several seconds he forgot he was in hiding. Forgot what was at stake. After all, this woman might have been involved in a conspiracy to commit murder. It was imperative he learn all he could about her.

And God knew he was learning plenty, given the way that drenched material clung to her. Clearly Mrs. Ralston had indulged in a dip in the hot springs. It was well documented that taking the waters was good for the body, and she was absolute testament to that.

She moistened her lips and his gaze was drawn to her mouth. Were her lips naturally so plush, or were they kiss-swollen? Had somebody joined her at the hot springs? An unexpected mental image flickered through his mind...of her, standing in the gently bubbling water...and of him, joining her—

Suddenly the object of his fantasies moved toward him. Simon's breath halted—partly due to the risk of discovery and partly because the sight of her rendered his lungs incapable of functioning. He'd seen many alluring sights in his life, but he'd be hard-pressed to name any that could compare to the sight of a wet, nearly naked Genevieve Ralston. He glanced down at the erection straining against his snug breeches.

And speaking of hard...

Blaze

Dear Reader,

Every once in a while a character, one who began as merely a friend of the hero or heroine, steals my heart and demands that their own story be told. Genevieve Ralston, who first appeared as a secondary character in my Regency-era historical *Love and the Single Heiress,* did just that. I've wanted to tell her story ever since she first appeared on the page—a woman who has fought to overcome both social and physical limitations. A woman who has known—and lost—love, and who never expects to feel it again. But when a handsome stranger calls upon her, she finds herself experiencing desires she'd believed long dead. However, there is much more to this man than she knows, and of course Genevieve has secrets of her own. And we all know where secrets can lead....

I hope you enjoy my first historical Harlequin Blaze novel—I had a great time writing about Genevieve and her handsome stranger's adventures. Perhaps their story will inspire you to enjoy some adventures of your own!

I love to hear from readers! You can contact me through my Web site at www.JacquieD.com, where you can find out about all my latest news.

Happy reading and adventuring,

Jacquie D'Alessandro

Jacquie D'Alessandro

TOUCH ME

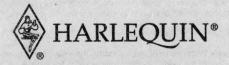

HARLEQUIN®

TORONTO • NEW YORK • LONDON
AMSTERDAM • PARIS • SYDNEY • HAMBURG
STOCKHOLM • ATHENS • TOKYO • MILAN • MADRID
PRAGUE • WARSAW • BUDAPEST • AUCKLAND

Recycling programs
for this product may
not exist in your area.

ISBN-13: 978-0-373-79499-7

TOUCH ME

www.eHarlequin.com

Printed in U.S.A.

ABOUT THE AUTHOR

Jacquie D'Alessandro is a *New York Times* and *USA TODAY* bestselling author of more than thirty books. She grew up on Long Island, New York, where she fell in love with romance at an early age. She dreamed of being swept away by a dashing rogue riding a spirited stallion. When her hero finally showed up, he was dressed in jeans and drove a Volkswagen, but she recognized him anyway. They now live out their happily-ever-after in Atlanta, Georgia, along with their son, who is a dashing rogue in the making. She loves to hear from readers and can be contacted through her Web site at www.JacquieD.com.

Books by Jacquie D'Alessandro

Don't miss any of our special offers. Write to us at the following address for information on our newest releases.

Harlequin Reader Service
U.S.: 3010 Walden Ave., P.O. Box 1325, Buffalo, NY 14269
Canadian: P.O. Box 609, Fort Erie, Ont. L2A 5X3

This book is dedicated to Brenda Chin with my gratitude for not only being a wonderful person and editor, but for seeing that Genevieve was a very special woman who deserved her own story. We both thank you for allowing me to bring her to life.

And, as always, to my wonderful husband, Joe, who fills my life with love and happiness, and our son, Chris, Fills My Life Junior.

1

Little Longstone, Kent, 1820

GENEVIEVE...*alabaster box...letter inside proves who did this...*

The Earl of Ridgemoor's dying words echoed through Simon Cooperstone, Viscount Kilburn's mind as he stealthily approached the cottage nestled among soaring elms, words the earl had gasped out with his last few breaths to Simon's urgent question: "Who shot you?"

With any luck, Simon was about to find out the answer—and catch the killer trying to frame him for the earl's murder.

The radical social reforms advocated by the earl—a man rumored to be the next prime minister—weren't universally popular. An attempt had been made on Ridgemoor's life two weeks earlier, an act Simon had already been investigating as part of his duties for the Crown. Now it was too late. Whoever had wanted Ridgemoor silenced had succeeded on their second attempt, something that filled Simon with a sick sense of guilt and failure.

Since becoming a spy for the Crown eight years ago, he'd suffered several unsuccessful missions, but none that had cast suspicion on Simon himself. Unfortunately, this failure had done just that—Ridgemoor's butler had discovered him standing over the earl's dead body, holding a pistol. Simon had gone to the earl's town house after receiving a note stating that Ridgemoor had important information to share. Sadly, Simon had arrived too late. The butler swore to the authorities that no one other than Simon had entered the house, and indeed, all the windows were locked from the inside.

When Simon saw the flickers of suspicion in his superior's eyes, he knew trouble was brewing. John Waverly, the man to whom he reported, hadn't *said* anything to indicate he doubted Simon's account, but Simon had sensed the man's hesitancy, and it had hurt more than he cared to admit. Eight years ago, Simon had known nothing about being a spy. In fact, he'd known nothing other than the wealth and privilege afforded him by his exalted title and family name. He'd wanted, needed, a change—needed to do something useful with his life—and John Waverly had taken him under his experienced wing and taught him the intricacies of the spy game. He'd always considered Waverly more than merely his superior—he admired and respected him, and thought of him as both a trusted friend and mentor.

As if Waverly's uncertainty didn't rankle enough, Simon also saw the glimmers of mistrust in the eyes of William Miller and Marc Albury, his two closest colleagues, men he thought of as brothers. Indeed, he often felt closer to Miller and Albury than he did to his own brother—Simon's spying activities weren't something he could confide to his family or friends. If Miller, Albury or Waverly were in an untenable situation like the one in which Simon now found himself, would he give them the benefit of the doubt, regardless of the evidence pointing toward their guilt? He liked to think so, but perhaps, in the face of such damning evidence, he'd doubt his friends as they were doubting him.

With both the king and the prime minister demanding the swift capture of Ridgemoor's murderer, Simon feared speed would take precedence over accuracy, and the wrong man—namely him—could hang for the crime, especially as there were no other leads or suspects. Based on the number of missions that had gone wrong over the past year, Simon, Miller, Albury and Waverly, as well as other colleagues, believed someone within their ranks was a traitor, but so far they'd been unsuccessful in discovering who. All Simon knew was that it wasn't him. Now, unfortunately, it appeared as if he stood alone in that knowledge.

Not knowing who he could trust, who had his best interests at heart, he had lied when asked if Ridgemoor had divulged anything to him. Since Waverly, as well as Miller and Albury could smell an untruth at twenty paces, Simon's prevarication had only made matters worse and deepened the suspicion he saw in their eyes. No charges had been leveled against him yet, but his instincts warned him it was only a matter of time. And that was why he needed the alabaster box Ridgemoor had spoken of. Now. So he could reveal the identity of the guilty party before he faced his own execution.

With time short, he'd asked Waverly for a leave to clear his name. His superior had studied him at length, then finally nodded and said, "I believe you've lied—and you'd better have a bloody good reason for it—but I don't think you killed Ridgemoor. Still, the evidence against you is damning and if the top demands your head, there won't be much I—or anyone else—will be able to do to help you. I'll give you a fortnight, Kilburn. I'll tell everyone you're recovering from a fever believed to be contagious—that should temporarily keep them away. Do what you have to do to clear your name, and for God's sake do it quickly. I'll work on this end to help you."

It was all Simon could ask for and he hadn't wasted any time. His investigations over the past two days since Ridgemoor's murder had led him here—to the home of Mrs. Genevieve Ralston, the woman who, until a year ago, had been Ridgemoor's mistress. Had Ridgemoor's final words meant Mrs. Ralston was involved in the plot to kill him? Or had she perhaps shot him herself? It seemed a good possibility.

Information Simon had ferreted out indicated that Ridgemoor had abruptly ended his decade-old arrangement with Mrs. Ralston a year ago. Could she be a woman scorned who'd sought revenge? Or could her motives be of a more political bent? Was she perhaps an enemy of the Crown, one who'd helped get rid of Ridgemoor before he could become prime minister?

According to Simon's sources Mrs. Ralston rarely left her property in the small country village of Little Longstone, and the earl had been murdered in London. But then, London was only a three-hour carriage ride away. What better ruse than to be a recluse and sneak away unseen to commit crimes?

Tonight, for instance, Mrs. Ralston had left her cottage five minutes ago. She had only one servant, a giant of a man named Baxter, who Simon had ascertained was currently sitting in a booth at the village pub, a tankard of ale in his hand. So long as Mrs. Ralston returned home before Baxter, no one would know she hadn't spent the evening in her cottage.

No one except whoever she may have gone to see. And Simon.

Standing in the deep shadows cast by the tall trees surrounding her home, Simon had watched her walk down the path which led to the hot springs on her property as well as to a pair of neighboring cottages. He'd learned that one of those homes was currently unoccupied, and the other had been let several months ago to an artist, Mr. Blackwell. Was Mrs. Ralston heading for the hot springs, or for a visit with the artist? Or did she have another destination in mind? Simon didn't know. And as much as he'd wanted to follow her, right now her cottage was empty and he needed to take advantage of the opportunity to find the alabaster box containing the proof that would clear his name.

Crouching low, he sprinted the short distance to the cottage. Slipping a thin strip of metal between the nearest French windows, he expertly finessed the tool over the lock. Good fortune was with him as clouds momentarily obscured the stars and moon, casting the area in unrelenting blackness, which suited his purposes perfectly.

He pulled in a slow, deep breath of cool air scented with the first hints of autumn, opened the window and slipped inside a well-appointed sitting room. As he searched, taking care to leave everything exactly as he found it, he noted that Mrs. Ralston had an excellent eye for furnishings and a weakness for artwork. Framed pieces adorned the cream-colored walls, everything from landscapes to sketches to framed poetry to portrait miniatures.

Based on what little he'd been able to find out about her since he'd first heard her name just two days earlier, Genevieve Ralston was not a rich woman, yet her possessions spoke of understated wealth. How could she afford such trappings? Gifts from a generous benefactor—or payment for murder?

A loud meow broke into his thoughts and he looked down. An enormous black-and-white cat stared up at him, its fluffy tail twitching.

"Are you friend or foe?" he murmured.

The cat rubbed its whiskers against his boots then twined its furry self between his feet.

"Friend, then." He crouched down to scratch behind the beast's ears and was rewarded with the loudest purr he'd ever heard.

"You like that, don't you." A smile pulled at his lips when the cat answered with what sounded like a feline sigh of bliss.

"You must be a lady. You're much too pretty to be a boy."

She flicked her tail and moved just out of his reach, then looked at him as if to say, "If you want to continue to pet me, you'll have to come over here."

A chuckle tickled Simon's throat. Definitely a female.

He stretched out his arm and gave the cat one last scratch, then rose. "As grateful as I am that you're not a large snarling dog, I'm afraid I have no more time for you."

Precisely. Time was ticking and the alabaster box was nowhere in the sitting room. He moved on to the dining room, library and morning room, with the cat following him, weaving between his legs at every opportunity. Artwork and finely crafted furniture filled each room, but he found nothing resembling the box he sought. Tamping down his frustration, Simon climbed the stairs and made his way to Mrs. Ralston's bedchamber. After closing the door behind him to keep out the overly curious cat, he glanced around, noting it was the most richly appointed room in the house. Moonlight now streamed in through the windows flanking the four-poster bed covered with a pale-green counterpane and accented with fluffy pillows. Opposite the bed was a dresser and an oval cheval glass. A massive carved-wood wardrobe and dressing screen occupied the far wall, while a feminine escritoire and a chintz-covered chair lined the other.

More framed artwork hung on the pale-gray walls, but the most striking object in the room was a life-sized statue of a woman wearing nothing save a secretive smile. She stood in the corner beside the escritoire, a reigning goddess of pure-white marble that glowed in the moonlight. One of her graceful hands extended outward in invitation, and Simon could almost hear her teasingly whisper *Touch me.* In her other hand, she held a bouquet of flowers between her breasts, the petals of one bloom curving to touch her nipple. She was so lifelike, Simon found himself tempted actually to touch her to assure himself she wasn't real.

Pulling his gaze from the statue, he crossed to the wardrobe. An examination of the contents revealed that Mrs. Ralston preferred simple yet exquisitely made gowns in fine materials and owned more bonnets and shoes than any woman could possibly require. His brows raised when he discovered a small, pearl-handled pistol tucked inside a boot in the back of the wardrobe. Clearly, in spite of living in a sleepy little village, Mrs. Ralston felt the need for protection. From what? Or whom? Did she fear for her safety because she was guilty of something—such as the death of her former lover?

So many questions regarding this woman...questions, he suspected, that would lead to the answers he sought regarding Ridgemoor's death, thereby proving Simon's innocence and saving his neck from the hangman's noose.

He continued on to the dresser. Several pale strands of Mrs. Ralston's blond hair were trapped in her brush. He lifted the cut-crystal perfume bottle to his nose and sniffed. She liked the scent of roses. Small ceramic pots on the dresser top contained an array of feminine creams and potions.

The first two drawers revealed dozens of pairs of gloves, in a dizzying variety of styles, materials and colors. Bloody hell, her weakness for shoes and bonnets didn't begin to compare with her apparent addiction to gloves. The other drawers revealed chemises and stockings so sheer they were nearly transparent. Simon well knew that the more sheer the underclothes, the more costly they were. Obviously Mrs. Ralston had done very well for herself. Because she traded in secrets and murder plots that impacted national security?

He slipped his hands beneath the filmy undergarments and stilled when his fingers brushed something hard. His pulse kicking with excitement, he slipped the object from its hiding place.

An alabaster box.

With a rush of satisfaction, he moved closer to the beam of silvery moonlight and turned the book-sized object in his hand. A quick examination revealed it wasn't an ordinary box, but a puzzle. Bloody hell. He'd opened boxes such as this—depending on the intricacy of the pattern involved, it could require anywhere from a few minutes to several hours to find the correct combination of moves to release the top.

He hoped like hell it would only require a few minutes.

Employing the calm patience that had served him well through the years, he pressed his fingers over the cool, smooth surface, searching for a panel that would slide. The previous boxes he'd opened had been made of wood inlaid with intricate designs, which had made finding the sliding panels a bit easier. This box, however, looked like a solid piece of alabaster and contained no markings other than the pale swirls of color that naturally occurred in the mineral.

Several minutes passed before he finally touched the right spot and a slim section of alabaster slid forward. He continued, painstakingly touching the box again and again until he discovered the next small section to slide into place.

For the next quarter hour, the only sound in the room was the ticking of the mantel clock as he turned the box over and over, working the intricate pattern of sliding pieces. Finally he slid the piece into place that released the top of the box. *At last.* The evidence he needed would, in mere seconds, be his. Simon drew a deep breath then slowly slid back the top panel.

And stared into an empty cavity.

He frowned, slipping his fingers all around the inside the chamber, but it was indeed empty. Bloody hell.

Where was the letter? The proof he needed to save his neck? His lips flattened into a grim line. It seemed clear that Mrs. Ralston had found the evidence before he could.

Why would she remove it? The fact that she must have done so certainly pointed directly toward guilt of some sort. Had she acted alone in the plot to kill Ridgemoor, or was she in collaboration with others? What role did she play in this circle of death closing in on him? And what the bloody hell would she have done with the information? Hidden it somewhere else in the house?

Another quick examination of the box confirmed his belief that no other opening existed. With a sigh of frustration and disgust, he slid the panels back into place, replaced the box among the sheer underclothes and closed the drawer.

What next? Where to look? His gaze landed on the night table, and he strode across the room. A bouquet of flowers in a small crystal vase rested on the table's polished wood surface, along with an oil lamp and a book. Simon peered at the title. *A Ladies' Guide to the Pursuit of Personal Happiness and Intimate Fulfillment* by Charles Brightmore.

Interesting. He'd noted that same title during his search of the library. There had recently been some scandal attached to the book he remembered, although he hadn't paid particular attention. Still, it was curious that Mrs. Ralston would possess two copies. Could the letter from the box be tucked inside? He picked up the volume and leafed through the pages, but unfortunately his hope was in vain. He was about to close the book when a phrase caught his attention and he frowned. *Tie up her man?*

Turning so he could better capture the light streaming through the window, he read: *Today's Modern Woman should not hesitate to insist upon getting what she wants, be it in the drawing room or in the bedchamber—even if she has to tie up her man to get it. Indeed, tying him up in the bedchamber will most assuredly lead to very intriguing results...*

Simon's brows shot upward. Clearly he'd been mistaken to assume that a ladies' guide would merely contain information about fashion and etiquette.

"No wonder there was a scandal," he murmured.

An image flashed through his mind...of his hands being tied with a silken cord to a bedpost. He couldn't see his captor's face, but her voice was ripe with sensual promise when she whispered, "You're going to give me everything I want."

He blinked and the image evaporated, leaving him feeling slightly stunned and—he winced and shifted— more than slightly aroused. Unable to stop himself, he flipped to a different page and read: *Today's Modern Woman must realize the importance of fashion in her quest for intimate fulfillment.* Simon nodded. Ah, yes. This is more like what he'd expected. *There are times to wear a fancy ballgown, times to wear a negligée and times to wear nothing at all...*

So much for what he'd expected.

Another image materialized in his mind, this one of the same woman who'd tied his hands, her face still blurry and indistinguishable, shrugging her negligée from her shoulders. The satin puddled at her feet, leaving her bare to his avid gaze. Coral nipples erect, the pale curls between her legs glistening, she stepped from the pool of material and walked slowly toward him with a sinful sway of her hips. "Where have you, been?" she whispered. "I've been waiting for you..."

Simon shook his head to dispel the sensuous image. Bloody hell, no wonder this book had caused such an uproar. He'd never read anything like it. Of course, he wasn't in the habit of reading ladies' guides. At least, he hadn't been, until now. Even as his mind ordered him to put down the damn book and resume his search, he found himself again turning the page. Just as he peered at the words he heard the unmistakable sound of a door opening then closing.

Bloody damn hell.

A feminine voice softly crooned, "Hello, sweet Sophia. Did you miss me?" Sweet Sophia answered with a loud meow. "I missed you, too. We'll play tomorrow. I'm tired and off to bed."

Double bloody damn hell.

2

Furious that he'd allowed himself to be so uncharacteristically distracted, Simon quickly replaced the book then glanced around the room. The only two exit possibilities were the door—not a viable option, or one of the two windows, offering at least a thirty-foot drop to the ground—not a healthy option. Besides the potentially fatal fall, he'd have to leave the window open and she'd know someone had been in her chamber. Of course, unless he moved his arse—immediately—she was going to discover that anyway.

Bloody aggravating woman. Why couldn't she have a nice balcony off her bedchamber? And have stayed away for several more hours?

Ignoring the screen and the wardrobe—both of which she'd undoubtedly use in the course of readying herself for bed, he moved swiftly toward the statue in the corner. He'd no sooner secreted himself in the deep shadows behind the marble woman than the bedchamber door opened.

Inwardly cursing the rotten luck that had brought Mrs. Ralston home so early, he remained still and prayed that she'd get into bed quickly and fall asleep immediately. From his hiding place, he watched her close the door behind her then move to the bedside table where she lit the oil lamp. Surrounded by a soft golden glow, she pushed back the hood on the dark cape she wore.

Simon blinked in surprise. Mrs. Ralston was much younger than he'd imagined. Based on the meager information he'd been able to gather in the short time he'd had to investigate, he'd discovered she'd retired from the life of being a mistress a year ago when Ridgemoor had ended their arrangement. That news had led Simon to assume she'd aged and lost her beauty. Between that and the fact that the earl was over fifty and she'd been his mistress for a decade, he'd envisioned a woman in her forties, at the least. But this woman didn't appear much older than thirty, if she was that.

And she certainly hadn't lost her looks. The woman standing before him in the halo of golden lamplight was nothing short of stunning. The combination of high cheekbones and full lips lent her an exotic yet delicate beauty. He couldn't tell what color her eyes were, but given her porcelain skin and upswept honey-blond hair, he'd wager blue. He found himself wondering if they'd more resemble a cloudless summer sky or a stormy sea. Or perhaps a shard of ice.

All thoughts of ice vanished in the next instant when she unfastened her cloak. The garment slid from her shoulders to reveal that she wore only a chemise. A *wet* chemise. A wet chemise that clung to her body as if it had been painted on her skin—with transparent paint.

Simon's breath halted, and for several seconds he completely forget where he was. Who she was. And how much was at stake. His conscience—an inner voice he'd bludgeoned into silence long ago—unexpectedly coughed to life and informed him that honor and decency demanded he avert his gaze. He immediately

consigned his conscience back to the depths from where
it had crawled and kept his eyeballs steadfastly trained
on the vision before him. After all, she was a person of
suspicion. For reasons he'd yet to discover, she'd taken
what he'd come to steal before he could rob her of it—
the letter that would save his life. It was imperative he
learn all he could about her.

And God knows he was learning plenty, given the
way that wet material clung to her. His gaze roamed
slowly downward, lingering over her firm, full breasts
topped with erect nipples. The curve of her waist flared
to generous hips then tapered to shapely thighs. The
curls between her legs were the same golden honey
shade as her hair.

Clearly Mrs. Ralston had indulged in a dip in the hot
springs. It was well documented that taking the waters was
good for the body, and she absolutely was testament to that.

She moistened her lips and his gaze was drawn to her
mouth. He squinted through the shadows. Were her lips
naturally so plush or were they kiss-swollen? Had
someone joined her at the hot springs? Did Mrs. Ralston
have a lover? Perhaps the artist from the neighboring
cottage? Or an accomplice who'd helped her murder
Ridgemoor? Surely a woman who looked like her
wouldn't lack for male companionship. An unexpected
mental image flickered through his mind…Mrs.
Ralston, standing in the gently bubbling water…and
himself, joining her—

"Meow."

The sound cut off Simon's unsettling fantasy and his
gaze jerked downward. Sophia slid into the shadows and
once again twined herself around his boots. Bloody
hell. Clearly the cat possessed the same unfortunate

habit as her owner—turning up in places she wasn't wanted. And wasn't that just like a female? Give one the smallest amount of attention then they kept pestering you for more.

He looked up and stifled a groan. With her cloak folded over her arm, Mrs. Ralston moved toward him. His breath halted—partly due to the great risk of discovery and partly because the sight of her rendered his lungs incapable of functioning. He'd seen many alluring sights in his life, but he'd be hard-pressed to name any that could compare to the sight of a wet, nearly naked Genevieve Ralston.

And speaking of hard…his gaze flicked down to the erection straining against his snug breeches. How bloody delightful. It was humiliating enough that he might very well be discovered. To be found in such a condition was completely unacceptable. He tried to will away his arousal, but with his gaze locked on her luscious form once again, he utterly failed. By God, Ridgemoor must have been jaded indeed to have tired of this woman. Had she sought revenge by murdering him?

Or perhaps he hadn't tired of her as rumors had suggested—perhaps she'd betrayed him and that had precipitated Ridgemoor's swift ending of their relationship. As Simon well knew, women could be perfidious creatures. And he had no doubt there was more to this particular woman than her simple existence as a former mistress who'd retired to the country. At the minimum, she possessed a box that contained information vital to Simon and many other people—or at least, it *had* contained that information, until the box had come into her possession. What possible reason other than guilt of some sort could have driven her to remove the letter?

She laid her cloak over the back of a wing chair near the fireplace and he held his breath. For several tension-filled seconds, she stood so close to him he had but to reach out his hand to touch her arm.

"What are you doing in the corner, Sophia?" she murmured. "I hope you haven't found a mouse."

No, not a mouse.

Sophia unwrapped herself from Simon's boots and trotted toward her mistress. After giving the cat an affectionate pat, Mrs. Ralston crossed to her dresser and removed a clean chemise from the drawer, while Sophia jumped onto the bed and settled herself in the center of the counterpane. Simon pulled in a slow, deep breath of relief, noting Mrs. Ralston had left behind a hint of her scent—the same soft rose fragrance that filled the crystal bottle on her dresser.

Standing with her back to him, she peeled the wet chemise down her body, giving a slow wriggle that had him clenching his hands. A fine layer of sweat misted his forehead and, although he continued to fight to control his body's reaction to her, it was a battle well and truly lost when she bent over to pick up the garment, a move that hiked her shapely bottom in the air and afforded him an unimpeded view of her feminine charms—a heart-stopping, concentration-destroying vision that drove every thought from his mind, including the fact that the verdict of *hanged by the neck until dead* could figure prominently in his near future.

As he gritted his teeth and bit back a groan, she pulled the fresh chemise over her head, then walked to the wardrobe and, thank God, pulled out a satin robe which she donned. The soft material clung to her curves like a second skin, but at least they were covered. He hoped now she'd go to bed.

Instead, she returned to the dresser and massaged cream from one of the pots into her hands, wincing several times as if in pain. Then she donned a pair of gloves from the top drawer. The ritual struck him as odd. Did all women wear gloves to bed? Any time he'd spent the night with a woman, he kept her too busy and too sated to think about anything as mundane as hand cream and gloves.

His hope that Mrs. Ralston would *now* retire was dashed when she reached up and pulled the pins from her hair, releasing a curtain of shimmering blond curls that fell to her hips. He immediately imagined running his hands through those spiral tresses, wrapping them around his fist. Pulling her closer—

He briefly squeezed his eyes shut to dispel the unexpected, unwanted image. What the hell was wrong with him? Bad enough he should be entertaining fantasies while on a mission, but it was completely unacceptable that he do so when the subject of those fantasies was a woman who well might be implicated in a deadly plot.

She emitted a low groan and his eyes snapped open to find her tying off the end of the braid she'd made with a pale blue ribbon while he'd been lustfully daydreaming. Before he could decide why she'd made such a sound, she again walked toward him. His every muscle tensed. Had she detected his presence? Sensed she was being watched? Bloody hell, it seemed as if she were staring directly at him. If she discovered him, he'd have no choice but to subdue her. A mental picture instantly formed in his mind…yet the vision wasn't of *him* subduing *her,* but rather of *her* tying *him*…with pale-blue ribbons. To her bed.

Damn it. That bloody *Ladies' Guide* had utterly corrupted his mind.

To his relief she settled herself on the dainty chair before her escritoire, but his ease quickly evaporated when she lit the single candle on the desk. Light flared and he shrank as far into the shadow cast by the marble statue as possible. What the bloody hell was she doing?

She silently answered his question when she withdrew a sheet of vellum from the drawer and reached for the quill pen. In spite of his wish that she'd retire so he could escape, Simon's interest quickened. She was going to write a letter. One that might provide him with vital information? It seemed an odd time to compose a missive—unless one was being secretive.

Simon watched her write smoothly for several minutes, but then her movements began to slow. Her brow furrowed and her lips pressed tightly together. She bent over the vellum with what he first assumed was concentration on her task, but then his gaze dropped to her hand that held the quill. She now gripped the instrument in an awkward manner. After writing several more words, she stopped then slowly flexed her gloved fingers as if she were in pain. Given her pinched expression, it was obvious something was amiss. Had she suffered some sort of accident that had damaged her hands?

She wrote with that same pained expression for another minute or two, then set the pen back in the holder and sanded the vellum. After slipping the paper into the drawer, she blew out the candle, rose and walked to her bed. He watched her remove her robe then extinguish the oil lamp. Bathed in a swathe of silver moonlight, she pulled back the counterpane and settled herself between the sheets. Sophia raised her head for several seconds, then resumed her curled-up position. Mrs. Ralston closed her eyes. She looked like an innocent angel—but Simon knew better than to accept outward appearances.

Soon he detected the sound of her slow, even breathing. He waited an additional few minutes, then, satisfied she was indeed asleep, he slipped from his hiding place and silently left the room. As he closed her front door behind him, he vowed that he would discover not only what Mrs. Genevieve Ralston had done with his letter and why, but what all her secrets were.

Especially whether those secrets included murder.

3

London is hectic and exciting, and married life is wonderful. The only thing missing is you, my dear friend. I wish you would come to town to visit…

THE WORDS of the letter blurred as tears flooded Genevieve Ralston's eyes, tears she quickly brushed away when she heard heavy footfalls in the corridor. Seconds later her giant of a manservant, Baxter, entered the sitting room.

"Wanted to let ye know that—" His words cut off, and setting his beefy fists on his hips, he narrowed his eyes. "Yer upset. Wot's wrong?" Before Genevieve could answer, his gaze dropped to the letter she held and understanding dawned in his dark eyes. "Yer sad from missin' yer friend Lady Catherine."

Genevieve swallowed the ball of misery tightening her throat and forced a light laugh. "A bit."

"More than a bit," Baxter said, his voice gruff. He studied her for several seconds with an expression that made her feel as transparent as glass. "Ye ain't been the same since she got married and moved to London. Been three months. I hate seein' ye so unhappy."

"I'm not unhappy," Genevieve said, walking to the desk and slipping the letter into a drawer. It was true, she told herself. She was merely lonely. Before Catherine had moved to London, hardly a day had gone by when they hadn't seen each other. But now…Catherine's absence left Genevieve floundering. The days that used to be filled with laughter, conversation and confidences with her best friend now echoed with silence and loneliness and far too much introspection. She now had too much time to think about Richard and the pain of being cast aside after ten years. The arrival of the puzzle box had only made things worse. As had his cryptic note: "You're the only one I can trust. Keep this safe and I will come for it as soon as I can."

That brief missive had struck her like a hard slap, leaving her confused and angry. Why hadn't he sent the box to the younger, exquisite mistress he'd replaced her with? She could still see the pity, and worse, disgust in his eyes when he'd looked at her imperfect hands the last time she'd seen him, when he'd rejected her touch and attempts to seduce him. Two days later, he'd abruptly ended their arrangement, without even the courage or the decency to tell her to her face. Instead he'd sent a curt note, along with a parting monetary gift. As if money could soothe the hurt and pain and humiliation.

Even now, a year after he'd discarded her, a part of her still couldn't quite believe that he'd been so unfeeling. So unkind. He'd told her he loved her. And she'd loved him—perhaps not at first, but soon after they'd met. At the beginning of what had turned into a decade-long affair, she'd merely been pitifully grateful to have found a way out of the desperate situation in which she'd found herself. She hadn't wanted to become a mistress, but given the alternatives, or lack thereof, Richard's offer had been nothing short of a miracle.

When she'd agreed to be his mistress, all she'd known was that he was wealthy, attractive and that he desired her—enough to save her from the nightmare her existence had become—and that was enough. She soon realized, much to her relief, that he was also kind. Generous. Intelligent. A progressive thinker who cared about the plight and sufferings of those less fortunate than himself and who hoped to bring changes to the laws to help the poor. She'd fallen in love with his character, his mind, his goodness. But his cold dismissal of her had shown her a side of him she'd never known existed, one that had made her feel like a fool. She'd felt ugly and dirty, and the day he'd discarded her she'd vowed she'd never be another man's mistress. Never let another man own her, especially a damned noblemen, one with the wealth and power to replace her within days with another lover. By God, if another nobleman looked at her with so much as a gleam in his eye, she'd set Baxter on him.

Well, she'd keep Richard's puzzle box safe until he came for it, although she'd wager he'd send someone in his stead, in which case she'd just keep the letter she'd discovered inside the box. She'd read the missive and couldn't fathom the importance of such an innocuous note. Perhaps it was a code of some sort, but she couldn't decipher it, and she really didn't care to know its significance. Richard would have to fetch the letter himself if he wanted it, as she was certain he did. She'd simply force him to do what he should have had the decency to do in the first place—face her. She'd pleasured him and shared herself with him for ten years and had foolishly fallen in love with him. He owed her that much.

She couldn't deny there was a small, petty part of her

that hoped he regretted his actions, that he wanted her back. But it didn't matter if he did. That part of her life was over. While she'd never allow herself be that vulnerable again, she was grateful that her years of financial support from Richard had enabled her to purchase this cottage and provide this sanctuary for herself and Baxter.

"Bloody hell," Baxter muttered, shaking his head. "I know ye better than anyone. I know yer miserable and nothin' I do seems to help. I'd like to pound that fancy bastard lordship to dust for wot he done to ye. 'Tis the way of the rich and titled to take wot they want then spit out wot's left over with no regard for anyone or anything 'cept their own selfish needs."

Guilt flooded Genevieve. Here she thought she'd successfully shown a brave face, but clearly she'd failed. Dear Baxter. He was the most loyal of friends and guarded her as if she were one of the crown jewels. They'd known each other since adolescence and had been through a great deal together, some of it very good, some of it very bad. She loved him like a brother. He credited Genevieve with saving his life years ago when, at age fifteen, he'd been left for dead in an alleyway behind the bordello where her mother plied her wares and Genevieve cooked and cleaned and prayed for a better life. Given her own precarious situation at the time, she knew she and Baxter had saved each other.

"I'm fine, Baxter," she said, proud of how sincere she sounded. "A bit lonely, I admit, but I'm adjusting." She shoved aside her conscience that informed her she was, in fact, miserably lonely and wasn't adjusting at all. "I appreciate your concern, but I assure you it's not necessary."

"Them tears in yer eyes say different," Baxter muttered with a fierce scowl that would have terrified anyone but Genevieve. Certainly no one would guess that this giant bald man with thighs that resembled tree trunks and fists the size of hams was as gentle as a kitten and baked the most delicious scones in the kingdom. Of course, he could also break a man's neck with his bare hands if necessary—something that never failed to make Genevieve feel safe and protected. A woman living on her own could never be too careful. Especially a woman with secrets…secrets that could potentially bring danger to her door.

She straightened her spine and met his gaze. "They are tears of happiness—for Catherine. Who is deliriously in love and thriving in London." Determined to change the subject, she said, "When you entered the room you mentioned there was something you wanted to let me know?"

It was clear by his mutinous expression that Baxter wanted to press his point. But after heaving a sigh that indicated he knew damn well she wasn't being entirely truthful, he said, "That bloke is here, askin' if yer at home."

"Bloke? What bloke?"

Baxter thrust a calling card at her. "The one wot rented Dr. Oliver's cottage."

Ah, yes. Baxter always knew the goings on in Little Longstone—not that there were many—and had mentioned that the Oliver cottage had been leased by some "bloke." Several months ago the good doctor had inherited an estate. He'd wasted no time packing up his wife and heading for greener pastures.

Genevieve took the card and perused the words. Mr. Simon Cooper. His direction, printed below his name, was in a respectable, although far from wealthy, section of London. Nothing out of the ordinary, yet her suspicions were immediately aroused. This was the second newcomer to the area recently—first Mr. Blackwell the artist, now this Mr. Cooper. Her thoughts instantly flew to the worry that always lingered in the back of her mind: did this stranger know something? Suspect? Had evidence of her activities come to light?

Clearly her concern showed in her expression because Baxter said, "I know that look. Ye think he's here because of yer writin's? Because of Charles Brightmore?"

Genevieve's stomach tightened at the mention of her "nom de plume." "Do you?"

Baxter scratched his bald head. "Doesn't seem likely. That matter was taken care of months ago with those newspaper articles. Everyone knows Charles Brightmore left England. No reason to look for him here." Baxter's expression collapsed into a fierce frown. "'Course if this bloke *is* sniffin' around for Charles Brightmore, ye can be sure I'll be breakin' his damn nose. I'll let no harm come to ye, Gen."

The tension tightening Genevieve's shoulders relaxed. "I know. And you're right—as far as anyone knows, Brightmore has left England with no plans to return."

Baxter nodded. "Still, always pays to be careful. But I hafta say, this bloke don't look like any sort of investigator type. Acts more like a damn lovesick suitor is what, movin' in just this mornin' and not wastin' any time to call on ye. Says he's come to introduce himself since ye'll be neighbors for the next two weeks." He flexed his sausage-sized fingers. "I were tempted to toss him out on his gift-bearing arse, but seein' as how yer *just a bit* lonely, I suppose I could resist the temptation if some company might make ye smile."

"It's always best to avoid arse-tossing, unless it's absolutely necessary," Genevieve said in her most serious voice. Then she raised her brows. "Gift-bearing?"

"Brought a bouquet of flowers with him." Baxter's lip curled. "Bloke should know a woman like you is worth diamonds."

Genevieve laughed. "And of course you wouldn't be the least suspicious of a man I've never met who called upon me bearing diamonds."

A sheepish expression momentarily softened Baxter's rough-hewn features. "Suppose I would be, now that ye mention it." Then his scowl returned. "But ye can't trust anybody nowadays. Bloke musta gotten wind of the fact that a beautiful woman lived here, so wot's the first thing he does? Comes callin' with flowers, that's wot."

Genevieve barely squelched the incredulous sound that rose in her throat at what Baxter was implying. "There's no need to worry about that." Indeed, that part of her life was over. She glanced down at her gloved hands and pressed her lips together. The doctors called her affliction arthritis. She called it the curse that had robbed her of the man she'd loved. The man who couldn't bear to have her less-than-perfect hands touch him. Why would another man look upon her affliction differently? The answer was, they wouldn't. It didn't matter if Mr. Simon Cooper, or anyone else, called upon her. She had no intention of ever allowing herself to be hurt again.

When she looked up she saw that Baxter's gaze had followed hers. There was no missing the flash of sympathy in his eyes as he looked at her gloves. She quickly clasped her hands behind her back. While she appreciated Baxter's concern, she damn well didn't want his pity.

"What does this Mr. Cooper look like?" she asked.

He raised his gaze back to hers and frowned. "Like a flower-carryin' bloke who should be tossed out on his arse."

"I see. What sort of flowers?"

"Roses."

Her favorite. Of course Mr. Cooper would have no way of knowing that.

Under normal circumstances, she would have told Baxter to inform Mr. Cooper she wasn't in. She didn't care much for socializing outside her small circle of friends, and except for occasional visits to the village, she kept to herself. With Catherine gone, however, circumstances were no longer normal. A visit with a bloke bearing roses might not be ideal, but at least it broke up what had turned into a monotony of dull, dreary, solitary days.

"You may show Mr. Cooper in," she told Baxter.

After Baxter quit the room, she rose and crossed to the window. Nostalgia and loneliness stabbed her at the sight of the golden leaves floating past the glass panes. Normally at this time of year, she'd be strolling through her beloved garden with Catherine, discussing which plants needed to be pruned back and what should be added in the spring. And she should be looking forward to Little Longstone's annual autumn festival tomorrow instead of wallowing in loneliness.

She heaved a sigh that fogged the glass. Leaning back, she wiped away the condensation and forced aside the unwanted envy that welled inside her. She was happy for Catherine, truly she was. This desperate, aching emptiness would subside. When her inner voice whispered that she was fooling herself, she lifted her chin and straightened her spine. Nonsense. She wasn't alone. She had Baxter. And Sophia. And today, she had Mr. Cooper. And that would simply have to be enough. She'd learned—very painfully—the price of wanting too much.

Of course, Mr. Cooper was most likely decrepit and in his dotage, letting a cottage in Little Longstone for the same reason many others did—the medicinal benefits of the hot springs. Like Genevieve's property, Dr. Oliver's had its own private spring which was undoubtedly the main attraction for Mr. Cooper. He probably sported a host of ailments about which he'd want to wax poetic. She gave a philosophical shrug. At least he was someone to talk to. Sophia was a good listener, but sadly not much of a conversationalist.

"Mr. Cooper to see ye" came Baxter's voice from the doorway. She turned then stilled at the sight of the very *un*decrepit Mr. Simon Cooper who was under no circumstances in his dotage. Indeed, she'd be astonished if he'd reached his thirtieth year. Rendered uncharacteristically mute by surprise, she simply stared at him, and he appeared just as nonplussed as she. Intense green eyes pierced her, spearing a heated tingle through her, and for several seconds she couldn't move, forgot how to breathe. The way he was looking at her…it was as if he knew her. But that was ridiculous. They'd never met. She would not have forgotten this man.

The strange spell she'd fallen under was broken when he walked toward her with an easy grace that made it abundantly clear he didn't suffer from any ailments. Indeed, this tall, handsome, broad-shouldered man was the healthiest-looking specimen she'd seen in a very long time, a fact that once again aroused her suspicions. Why would he lease a cottage in an obscure village like

Little Longstone rather than in the much more fashionable Brighton or Bath?

He stopped in front of her and made her a formal bow. "Mrs. Ralston," he said, in a deep, slightly husky voice. "Simon Cooper. Your new neighbor, at least for the next fortnight. Delighted to make your acquaintance."

Genevieve found herself staring into those compelling green eyes that held a hint of something she couldn't decipher…something that inexplicably rushed fire through her body, heating places that hadn't been warm for ages. Surely the flush she felt was only because he'd caught her off guard and not from any real attraction on her part—or his. She glanced down at her gloved hands. She was past all of that.

Regaining her aplomb, she inclined her head. "Likewise, Mr. Cooper."

He offered her the bouquet of pink roses he held. "For you." He smiled, drawing her attention to his mouth. His very lovely mouth. The sort of mouth that managed to look firm and soft, serious and sensual, all at the same time. His perfectly formed lips looked as if they knew how to kiss. Extremely well.

After a brief hesitation, she reached for the flowers, taking care, as she did with everyone, to avoid touching him. He moved his hand, however, and her fingers brushed against his, stilling her. Warmth penetrated the thin layer of her gloves, shooting a tingle up her arm, one that surprised and unsettled her. She hadn't felt that sort of flutter in a very long time. Pulling her hand away, she stepped back several paces. "Thank you," she murmured. "I'm very fond of roses."

Needing several seconds to collect herself, she crossed the Turkish carpet and tugged the bell cord for

Baxter. When he appeared in the doorway almost instantly, Genevieve buried her nose in the flowers to hide her smile. Clearly he'd been standing in the corridor, most likely waiting to see if he'd need to toss their gentleman caller into the privet hedges.

"A vase for these, please Baxter," she said, handing him the flowers. She turned to her guest. "Would you like some tea, Mr. Cooper?"

"That would be lovely, thank you."

She shot Baxter, who was alternately glaring at the roses and Mr. Cooper, a warning look. After one last fulminating glower, Baxter quit the room.

When she turned back to Mr. Cooper, she found him staring at the now-empty doorway with an amused expression. "I believe your butler was trying to incinerate me with his eyes."

"He's very protective."

His gaze returned to her and his lips twitched. "Indeed? I hadn't noticed."

The fact that Mr. Cooper found Baxter amusing rather than intimidating further piqued her curiosity. She moved to the grouping of chairs in front of the hearth where a cheery fire crackled. "Please join me," she invited, seating herself in her favorite wing chair and indicating the settee opposite her.

"Thank you."

She watched him settle himself, noting the way his midnight-blue jacket accentuated his broad shoulders and how his fawn breeches and polished black Hessians hugged his long, muscular legs. Whatever else Mr. Cooper might or might not have to recommend him, he was certainly very nicely made.

She lifted her gaze and found him regarding her with

an intensity that would have caused a less self-pos-
sessed woman to squirm. If she were still capable of
blushing, her cheeks most likely would have burned at
being caught looking him over so thoroughly. Instead
she returned his gaze measure for measure. Surely a
man who looked like him was accustomed to feminine
attention.

"What brings you to Little Longstone, Mr. Cooper?"

"A brief holiday. My employer recently married and
has taken a wedding trip to the continent." Mischief
glittered in his eyes and one corner of his mouth tilted
upward. "I cannot imagine why he didn't want me to accompany him, but there you have it. I decided to use the
opportunity to get away myself."

Hmm. Genevieve realized he was teasing, still, she'd
guess that his employer wouldn't want this shockingly
attractive man anywhere near his new wife.

"And what made you choose Little Longstone?"

"Dr. Oliver is an acquaintance and very kindly
offered me the use of his cottage. I'm looking forward
to relaxing in all this clear, country air."

"That was very generous of him. I hope Dr. Oliver is
faring well?"

"Very well indeed. His wife is expecting their first
child this spring."

Genevieve smiled. "How lovely. I shall have to
write to congratulate them. Tell me, what do you do
in London?"

"I am steward to Mr. Jonas-Smythe. Perhaps you've
heard of him? He is of the Jonas-Smythes of Lancashire."

Genevieve shook her head. In order to better converse
with Richard she'd once kept up with all the names and
doings of London's elite, but no more. "I'm afraid not.

I've never been to Lancashire and haven't traveled to town for several years."

"You were raised in Little Longstone?"

"No." If she *had* been raised in this quiet, lovely village, her life would surely have been much different. "I settled here a number of years ago."

"And what made you choose Little Longstone?"

She saw no harm in telling him the truth. "Mostly the proximity to the springs. I find them therapeutic. I also fell in love with the surroundings—the woods and quiet village."

"And what of Mr. Ralston? Does he enjoy the springs as well?"

She hesitated. Both the question and his demeanor were perfectly natural, yet something gave her pause. The intensity of his gaze perhaps? A slight edge to his voice? Yes, there seemed to be a bit of both. Could his query be more than mere friendly curiosity or casual conversation? It seemed so. Indeed it seemed…could his interest in the answer be…personal? Did he find her…attractive?

She instantly shoved the ridiculous notion aside. Surely she was mistaken. Heavens, it had been so long since she'd been in the company of a handsome young man she'd completely forgotten how to read the signals gentlemen tossed out.

"I'm afraid Mr. Ralston is…gone." They were the same words she always murmured when asked about her husband as they were true. She didn't like to tell boldfaced lies unless it was absolutely necessary. Mr. Ralston *was* gone—because he'd never existed. She'd only loved one man in her life, and Richard had never offered marriage. Of course, she'd known men didn't marry their mistresses, especially men of the peerage. Titled gentlemen might give their hearts to their bed partners, but they gave their name only to women of their own social class. Assuming the role of a widow had lent her the respectability necessary to fit in here in the quiet village she'd chosen to make her home. And after Richard had cast her aside, she had indeed felt like a widow who'd lost her life's partner.

"Gone?" Mr. Cooper repeated. "You mean for the afternoon?"

Obviously the bold-faced lie was necessary. Genevieve shook her head. "No. He passed away."

His expression turned solemn. "I'm sorry for your loss."

"Thank you. It happened years ago."

"Years ago?" he repeated softly. His gaze skimmed over her and when his eyes once again met hers, her breath caught at the unmistakable interest and admiration glimmering in the green depths. "You must have married as a child."

A tingle she'd last felt long ago rushed through Genevieve and this time she knew she wasn't wrong. Clearly just because she'd been out of the game for an extended period didn't mean she'd forgotten how to play.

Mr. Cooper was flirting with her.

The realization stunned her. Intrigued her. It was so long since a man had shown that sort of interest in her. The last man had been Richard—

Reality returned with a slap and her gaze dropped to her gloved hands. Richard hadn't wanted her to touch him any more. She'd learned her lesson. Learned it well. Whatever stirrings of attraction Mr. Cooper might be feeling would quickly die if he saw the imperfections her gloves hid.

Genevieve raised her gaze back to his and cleared her throat. "We weren't married very long before he passed. And you Mr. Cooper—are you married?"

"No. I travel a good bit with my work for Mr. Jonas–Smythe, so I'm not in one place long enough to form deep attachments." A slow grin that could only be described as devilish curved his lips. "So far no woman will have me."

Genevieve barely suppressed the incredulous "Ha!" that rose in her throat. She didn't doubt that as many women as he wanted had had him—in any way he chose to be had. He'd most likely left a trail of broken hearts in his wake. The unmarried ladies of Little Longstone would buzz around Mr. Cooper like bees to a hive. Which of them might lose their heart to this devastatingly attractive man? She didn't know. But she would not be one of them.

4

RELIEF washed through Genevieve when Baxter entered the room bearing a tray holding the silver tea service, and a platter filled with scones, clotted cream and her favorite raspberry jam. Mr. Cooper had unnerved her in a way that both intrigued and confused her, and she welcomed the respite of Baxter's presence.

After setting everything on the table in front of her, Baxter then proceeded to pour the tea, his huge hands handling the delicate china far more efficiently than she could. When he finished, he rose to his full height and cracked his knuckles.

"Will ye be needin' anything else?" he asked Genevieve, shooting Mr. Cooper a glowering scowl. Mr. Cooper smiled in return, which only darkened Baxter's expression further.

"No, thank you, Baxter."

Baxter headed toward the door, his heavy footfalls rattling the porcelain on the mantel. "Holler if ye need me. I'll be close by." With that he quit the room.

"Clearly if I'm foolish enough to give you any reason to 'holler,' I shall find my innards in Baxter's large hands," Mr. Cooper said in a very serious tone.

"Your innards would indeed become *out*ards," Genevieve agreed, indicating he should help himself to sugar or cream for his tea.

"As you stated, he's very protective," Mr. Cooper said, his gaze not wavering from hers as he dropped a sugar lump into his steaming tea. "But then, he should be. He has a great deal to protect."

Another wave of heat suffused Genevieve, this one annoying her. At two and thirty, she was far past the age for her head to be turned by a man's flattery. *It's been a long time since a man has flattered you,* her inner voice whispered.

Yes, obviously that was the problem. She suddenly realized that other than Baxter, she hadn't been alone with a man since Richard had tossed her aside like yesterday's trash. And there was no denying Mr. Cooper was extremely attractive. No wonder she felt so uncomfortably warm. And uncharacteristically tongue-tied.

She watched him add four more lumps of sugar to his tea—so many that the liquid nearly spilled over the top, and her lips twitched. "You like a bit of tea with your sugar, Mr. Cooper?" she asked, lifting her cup to her lips to hide her smile.

He lifted his cup and regarded her steadily over the rim. "I confess I've a weakness for sweets. Do you?"

"I suppose, although my preference is for Baxter's raspberry jam. You must try it."

She watched him spread the clotted cream and jam on a scone. His hands were browned by the sun, large and capable-looking, his fingers long and strong. The faint remnants of an ink stain marred his index finger, no surprise given his profession. He obviously spent many hours filling in columns of numbers to keep his employer's accounts.

An image flashed in her mind...of those masculine hands sifting through her hair, scattering pins, holding her head immobile as he leaned forward to brush those lovely firm lips over hers. Then his hands drifting lower—

"Don't you agree, Mrs. Ralston?"

The question, asked in his deep voice, popped the sensual picture like a soap bubble. Good heavens, what on earth was *wrong* with her? Her thoughts never wandered like that. He was gazing at her with an expectant expression. Clearly he'd asked her something... something he wondered if she agreed with. To her chagrin she had no earthly idea what that something was.

"Agree?" she murmured, her outwardly cool demeanor at complete odds with the heat racing through her.

"That we should indulge our weaknesses."

She watched, transfixed, as he took a bite from his scone and slowly chewed. Recalling herself, she opened her mouth to speak, but her words evaporated in what felt like a puff of steam when he swallowed then licked a bit of jam from his lips. That tiny flick of tongue reverberated through her as if he'd licked her lips rather than his own and to her consternation, she found herself involuntarily mirroring his action. His gaze dropped to her mouth and fire flared in his eyes.

"I...I suppose that depends on what one's weaknesses are," she murmured. Dear God, was that breathless sound her voice? "And if they are within one's means."

His gaze returned to hers. "Meaning?"

"If one harbors a weakness for diamonds but not the means to purchase them, well, then that is a weakness that should not be indulged."

"Lest one finds oneself deeply in debt."

"Or in Newgate for stealing."

"Are diamonds a weakness of yours, Mrs. Ralston?"

She thought of the stunning necklace and matching earbobs Richard had given her, trinkets she'd sold soon after he'd left her. "No. In fact, I don't really care for them. I find them cold and lifeless. I much prefer sapphires, although I wouldn't call them a weakness."

"What *would* you call a weakness?"

She considered fobbing off the question with a light laugh then changing the subject. But if she did, she wouldn't be able to ask him what his weaknesses were. And she very much wanted to know.

"Flowers," she answered. "Especially roses."

"Any particular color?"

"Pink is my favorite."

He smiled into her eyes and her breath hitched. Dear God, he was beautiful when he was serious, but when he smiled…*oh, my.* "I'm delighted that I brought you not only your favorite flower, but in your favorite color. What else?"

It took her several seconds to recall what they were discussing. Then she cleared her throat. "Cats. Books. Artwork."

He nodded and glanced around the room. "You've some lovely pieces." He tilted his chin toward the painting hanging over the mantel. "That piece, in particular, is remarkable. It's so vivid I can almost feel the sea spray hitting my face."

Genevieve glanced at the painting she'd created, at the swirling waves crashing against the rocks, and recalled the first time she'd touched a paintbrush to canvas as a young girl, so filled with hope, her hands free of the arthritis that would strike her years later as an adult, stunting her talent and leading to heartbreak.

Her gaze strayed to the woman standing at the top of the cliffs amidst a profusion of swaying wildflowers. She faced the tumultuous waters, her features indistinguishable, yet Genevieve knew who she was. Or at least who she was supposed to be.

"Thank you. It's a particular favorite of mine."

He rose and moved to the mantel, leaning forward to more closely examine the painting. "The pattern of brushstrokes is very unusual," he said.

Genevieve's brows rose. He showed unexpected knowledge for a steward. "You are a student of art?"

He hesitated for several seconds, then turned to smile at her over his shoulder. "In so far as Mr. Jonas-Smythe enjoys adding to his collection, I therefore need to know something of the subject." He returned to his seat. "The painting isn't signed."

"No." She'd never signed any of her work, a matter of discretion as Richard had placed many of her pieces in his homes.

"Where did you get it?"

"It was a gift." To herself, which made the statement true, although not completely truthful. But then she had no intention of telling him the truth.

His attention shifted to the doorway and she followed his gaze. Sophia meandered into the room, tail high, every line of her proclaiming that this was her house and those within it were fortunate that she allowed them to be there.

"It appears your mention of a weakness for cats was overheard," he said.

"That's Sophia. I'm afraid she's rather shy…"

Her words trailed off as her pet, who usually couldn't be bothered with strangers unless they offered her food, trotted toward Mr. Cooper as if a rasher of kippers hung around his neck. To Genevieve's surprise, Sophia jumped onto Mr. Cooper's lap without hesitation. She batted his lapel with her front paw, twitched her fluffy tail under his nose, then settled herself across his thighs as if he were her own personal mattress. Looking across at Genevieve through squinty eyes, she kneaded her front paws against Mr. Cooper's breeches and purred so loudly, it sounded as if three cats were in the room.

Mr. Cooper cleared his throat. "Um, yes, I can see she is extremely shy." When he lightly scratched her pet's head, Sophia closed her eyes and stretched her neck into his touch.

Genevieve stared in amazement. "She's *never* behaved like that with a stranger before. It's almost as if she knows you."

He shrugged lightly. "Animals like me."

Good Lord, the sight of his long, strong fingers stroking her cat caused flutters in Genevieve's belly.

"Tell me more about your weaknesses," he said.

She forced her gaze away from that stroking hand. More of her weaknesses? She dared not. Especially as it appeared she had one for him. "I've already confessed mine. It's your turn."

Petting the sleepy-eyed cat with one hand, he sipped from his tea with the other, his gaze never leaving hers. His unwavering regard flustered her in a way she refused to show. Yet for all her outward serenity, her insides quivered with something she'd thought long forgotten, but had felt enough times in the past to know without a doubt what it was.

Desire.

Desire she wouldn't, couldn't, *refused* to act upon, and therefore desperately didn't want to feel. Which meant she needed to end this impromptu tea party as soon as possible and send her far-too-attractive guest on his way. Still, to send him off *too* abruptly would no doubt make him wonder why, question whether she might have any interest in him.

Ten minutes. She'd give him ten more minutes. That was enough time not to appear rude or raise questions. She could endure his company and keep her unexpected, unwanted desire hidden for ten more minutes.

"We share a weakness for books," he said.

"Oh? What do you enjoy reading?"

"Anything. Everything. I recently read *Frankenstein* and found it fascinating. Shakespeare and Chaucer are favorites. As I'm not accustomed to all this quiet in the country, I fear I'll run out of reading material before my stay in Little Longstone is over."

"I've a good number of books. Before you leave, you're welcome to borrow several from my collection." The instant the words left her lips she regretted them. What was she thinking? Borrowing books would require another visit to return them.

"A very generous offer. Thank you. What do you like to read?"

"Like you, anything and everything. Sir Walter Scott. The poetry of Blake, Lord Byron and Wordsworth. The gothic novels of Mrs. Radcliffe. I recently finished reading Gibbon's *Decline and Fall of the Roman Empire*."

His brows rose. "Quite a departure from Mrs. Radcliffe's novels."

"Indeed. However, I enjoy variety."

"'Variety's the very spice of life, that gives it all its flavor,'" he quoted softly.

Genevieve's heart lurched. The husky timbre of his

voice made it sound as if he were discussing something far more intimate than poetry.

"William Cowper," she murmured.

"One of my favorite poets."

"One of mine as well."

"It appears we have quite a bit in common, Mrs. Ralston."

Genevieve ignored the blatant interest she heard in his voice. Saw in his eyes. "Clearly you like cats."

"I like animals of all sorts."

"Do you have any pets?"

"Not at this time, but I have had in the past. I am considering getting myself a dog."

"Then you should plan to attend the annual Autumn Festival in the village tomorrow. In addition to booths filled with food and trinkets and crafts, there are always several families with litters of puppies for sale."

"An excellent idea. I'll go—if you'll accompany me."

Genevieve firmly ignored the way her heart leapt. She opened her mouth to refuse, but before she could do so, he continued, "Choosing a dog is a serious decision, one that requires a second opinion." His eyes glittered with deviltry. "You wouldn't want me to pick out the wrong dog, would you?"

"There will be dozens of people at the festival who can help you choose."

"Perhaps. But I'd much prefer your opinion."

"And why is that?"

He finished the last sip of his tea, set the empty cup on the table, then, with a hand on Sophia's back to keep her in place, he leaned forward. A mere three feet separated their faces and she could see the fine grain of his skin. The thickness of his eyelashes. The tiny scar in the center of his chin. "I could say it's because you're familiar with the village and its residents, including those with puppies. I could also claim it's because you're intelligent. And both of those would be perfectly true. But in the name of honesty, I must confess I also have a weakness for beautiful, well-read women."

"I see. And you think to disarm me with flattery?"

A slow smile curved his lips and Genevieve had to press her own lips together to prevent herself from heaving a gushy feminine sigh. "Honesty, rather than flattery, was my weapon of choice. I also think we'd enjoy each other's company. I know I'd enjoy yours. Will you accompany me?"

Genevieve knew she should say no. Nothing could come of this flirtation other than her longing for something she couldn't have. Why torture herself? A flirtation with him, with any man, would ultimately lead to the same rejection she'd suffered with Richard.

Wouldn't it?

The fact that she asked herself that question stunned her, and with a jolt, she realized that the temptation of this attractive man's company was simply too strong a lure to ignore. It had been so long since she'd felt these flutterings. Since she'd felt attractive. Since she'd experienced even the tiniest flicker of hope that she might again experience any sort of physical intimacy. Of course, she'd never allow things to progress that far. But that didn't mean she couldn't enjoy his attentions, just for a little while.

"I'll meet you in the village square at noon," she said for a compromise. As he'd finished his tea and the ten minutes she'd allotted had passed, she asked, "Before you leave, I'll show you my library."

"Thank you." His slow smile warmed her. "And I'll look forward to tomorrow."

Genevieve rose, and, after gently setting Sophia on the carpet, he stood as well. His clear reluctance to depart wrapped another layer of warmth around her. She escorted him to her cozy library, remaining in the doorway while he perused her collection. After several minutes he returned to her bearing three books. "I appreciate the loan," he said. "I'll take very good care of them."

She escorted him to the foyer where a glaring Baxter thrust Mr. Cooper's hat at him.

"Thank you, Baxter," Mr. Cooper said, giving his slightly dented hat a look. He then shot Genevieve a quick smile and made her a formal bow. "Until tomorrow, Mrs. Ralston."

Genevieve watched him walk down the flagstone path leading from the cottage and barely suppressed a sigh. The man looked as good leaving as he did arriving.

"Until tomorrow?" Baxter asked, cocking a brow. "He's plannin' to visit again?"

"We're meeting at the Autumn Festival in the village. He's looking to acquire a dog and asked for my help."

"He thinks yer a veterinarian?"

Genevieve laughed. "No. Just an animal lover."

"Bloke wants more than yer help," Baxter muttered. "I saw the way he looked at ye."

"How was that?"

"Like he were a starvin' beast and ye had a mutton chop tied around yer neck."

A shivery tingle raced through Genevieve. Yes, she'd noticed that as well. Surely she shouldn't find that so…intriguing. Or arousing.

"I'm not sure I trust the bloke around ye."

"You don't trust anyone."

"I trust *you*," Baxter said. "Ain't sure about him. But since ye don't look as sad as ye did before he arrived, I suppose I'll hold off on the arse-tossin'."

"Don't worry, Baxter. I don't intend to see him again after tomorrow's festival." Genevieve headed back toward the sitting room. When she passed the library, curiosity had her entering and walking to the shelves. Which of her books had he borrowed? Perusing the volumes, she smiled when she noted that *The Mysteries of Udolpho* by Mrs. Radcliffe was missing, as was the final volume of Gibbon's *Decline and Fall of the Roman Empire*. When she saw the third empty space, however, her smile faded.

Why had Mr. Cooper borrowed *A Ladies' Guide to the Pursuit of Personal Happiness and Intimate Fulfillment* by Charles Brightmore?

The suspicions she'd pushed away earlier came back with a sickening crash, knotting her stomach with dread, a sensation she'd learned not to ignore. Especially considering that only a few months ago, someone had wanted Brightmore dead over the furor that had erupted over his scandalous writings promoting sexual independence for women. Was it possible that Charles Brightmore's rumored departure for America hadn't ended the threats against him?

She could only pray it wasn't so, because Charles Brightmore lived right here in Little Longstone. Indeed, she saw the fictional man every morning when she looked in the mirror. Was her secret identity as the author of the scandalous tome that had shocked society in jeopardy of being uncovered?

She pressed her hands to her midriff and drew a deep

breath. Dear God, was it possible there was more to Mr. Cooper's visit to Little Longstone, to her cottage, than he'd admitted? Was it possible he knew, or suspected who she was? Had he been hired to locate Charles Brightmore? Or worse—*harm* Brightmore?

She didn't know, but she was determined to find out.

5

THE NEXT afternoon, after checking to make certain he was unobserved, Simon departed Mrs. Ralston's cottage and headed swiftly down the path toward the village. Pulling his watch from his waistcoat pocket, he glanced at the time. Nearly one o'clock, almost an hour past the time he'd agreed to meet her. He slipped the timepiece back in his pocket and quickened his pace.

After watching her and Baxter leave the cottage at a quarter 'til noon, he'd slipped inside and continued his search for the letter. Unfortunately he'd been no more successful than he had during his last hunting expedition. He'd wanted to remain longer, but he dared not lest she return home and catch him where he wasn't supposed to be.

Bloody hell, what had she done with that damn letter?

If only her cat Sophia could talk. The animal had followed him from room to room, rubbing against him and purring loudly. When he'd scratched behind her ears and asked where his letter might be hidden, Sophia had merely leaned into his hand and purred louder. And Simon had asked himself the question he most didn't want to— What if Mrs. Ralston had destroyed the letter?

With grim determination, he'd headed toward her bedchamber, telling himself that if that were the case, then he'd just have to return to London, continue his investigation, and convince Waverly, along with Miller and Albury, of his innocence and that he needed their help to prove it. Surely, on a gut level, his mentor and two closest friends knew Simon wasn't guilty. Someone, somewhere, knew something, knew the truth, and by God if the letter was lost to him, Simon would find that something.

Searching Mrs. Ralston's bedchamber again, he'd hated himself for the way his hands lingered over her clothing, her perfume bottle. Never in his life had he been so overwhelmed with lust, and definitely never during an investigation. The fact that he felt such staggering desire for a woman whose innocence was suspect truly grated on him. Bloody hell, he'd stolen one look at her in that wet chemise and taken leave of his senses. Throughout his search he'd had to force himself to concentrate on the task at hand, on finding the letter—the letter that would save his life.

Still, while he hadn't found the missive, he *had* discovered something very unexpected. Curiosity regarding what she'd been writing the night he'd hidden in her bedchamber had propelled him to her escritoire. Snatches of words written on the stack of vellum sheets he'd found in the top drawer of her desk drifted through his mind.

Today's Modern Woman should not hesitate to seduce her man… Today's Modern Woman must master the art of removing her gentleman's clothing—and her own…Today's Modern Woman will greatly benefit from discreetly brushing her body against her gentleman's in a crowded ballroom, then "accidentally" stroking her hand over the front of his breeches…

The handwriting had started smoothly, but had degenerated into an increasingly cramped jumble of letters. Last night he'd read *A Ladies' Guide to the Pursuit of Personal Happiness and Intimate Fulfillment* by Charles Brightmore and although the writing style and mention of Today's Modern Woman were identical to the pages he'd found in Mrs. Ralston's desk, nothing in the published book matched what she'd written on those pieces of vellum. Therefore, Mrs. Ralston was either very closely connected to Charles Brightmore—or Brightmore was merely a "nom de plume," and she was the author of the book. And working on a second volume.

His instincts told him the latter was the case. He recalled that several months ago there had been a great deal of interest in the mysterious Charles Brightmore. The author had never shown himself in society or at any literary gatherings. Simon vaguely remembered talk of threats against the man whose *Ladies' Guide* had incensed the gentlemen of the ton for its radical ideas on women's independence. The last he'd heard, Brightmore had left the country.

But Simon would wager everything he owned that Brightmore hadn't left the country at all. That the reason he'd never shown himself was because *he* was a *she*. And that *she* was Genevieve Ralston.

Very interesting.

As was the information contained in the explicit book. Frankly, he'd never read anything like it. Under the guise of an innocent guide for ladies, Genevieve Ralston had provided an arsenal of detailed information on carnal relations that only a very sexually experienced woman could provide. He'd found the information fascinating. Stimulating. And damned arousing—even more so now that he suspected his beautiful and mysterious neighbor had secretly written it.

Certainly that information would prove useful. All he wanted was his damn letter, so he could return to London and clear his name, regain his reputation with Waverly, Miller and Albury. He'd do whatever was necessary to get the letter, and now he had the ammunition to do so. He wasn't above resorting to blackmail. Not that he had any desire actually to tell anyone her secret, but *she* didn't know that. Yet, given her obvious experience in the bed-chamber, it would be much more civilized—and pleasur-able—for him to simply seduce the information from her.

Yes, that was an excellent plan—seduce her, then get her to confide the whereabouts of the letter. He'd begin by flirting today, then coaxing her into his bed as soon as possible.

The same image that had haunted him since the night he'd read that tantalizing snippet of the *Ladies' Guide* in her bedchamber…of her, wet and naked, tying him to her bed, flashed through his mind. Of her beautiful, lush body brushing against his. His tongue exploring all the places his bound hands couldn't touch…

His rapid footsteps faltered on the path to the village and he halted. Damn it, his skin felt hot and tight and his lungs pumped like a bellows—and not because of any physical exertions. He glanced down and glared at the erection pressing against his snug breeches. Bloody hell. Every time he thought of the woman his damn cock swelled. And he'd thought of her more times than he cared to count since seeing her in that damn wet, transparent chemise. Clearly seducing her wouldn't present any hardship—his body could hardly wait.

Which thoroughly vexed and confused him. Even

the knowledge that she'd removed the letter that, according to Ridgemoor's last words, would name his murderer and thereby clear Simon's name didn't cool his ardor. What the bloody hell was *wrong* with him?

Wincing, he adjusted himself, buttoned his coat—thank God the weather was cool enough to require one—then once again resumed walking. Several minutes later he arrived at the outskirts of the village. The humming mixture of voices, singing, music and shrieks of children's excited laughter grew louder as he approached, as did the savory scents of a variety of foods.

Pausing in the shadow cast by a tall brick building, Simon surveyed the scene. Dozens of bright awnings surrounded the large village square, with vendors calling out to the passersby in hopes of tempting them with their wares. Several hundred people, certainly more than he'd expected, milled about, purchasing trinkets and household items, sampling food and drinks. On the far side of the square an area had been cleared where a group of children chased each other about in circles. A quartet of musicians played, filling the cool air with their lively tune.

His gaze searched the crowd, halting, along with his breath, when it found Mrs. Ralston standing across the square. Dressed in a cornflower-blue pelisse and matching bonnet, she stood in a bright pool of sunshine, smiling up at her giant of a manservant. To Simon's annoyance, his every muscle tensed with want and his heart performed some sort of acrobatic maneuver—the same odd rollover he'd experienced when he'd called upon her yesterday and seen her for the first time up close and in the daylight.

No doubt about it, Genevieve Ralston was exquisite.

Flawless porcelain skin, huge sky-blue eyes, delicate features, full lips, honey-blond hair—he could easily understand why Ridgemoor had kept her as his mistress, and again he wondered why the earl had tired of such a beautiful woman—a question that truly perplexed him now that he knew, through her writings in the *Guide,* of her expertise in the bedchamber. He'd entered her sitting room yesterday afternoon and the sight of her had hit him like a blow to the midsection. He'd experienced hard punches of lust before, but never like that. Never on such a primal, visceral level. Surely it was only due to the fact that he'd seen her in that sodden chemise, an image that was branded in his mind.

Yet even as he told himself that, he couldn't deny there was something about her, something he couldn't quite put his finger on, that threw him off balance. Perhaps it was the unexpected air of vulnerability he sensed. He could see it in her eyes, that and a hint of hesitancy, of self-consciousness that he wouldn't normally equate with such an experienced woman. The fact that she'd been surprised when he'd flirted with her intrigued and puzzled him. Oh, she'd regained her aplomb quickly, yet there was no missing how he'd disconcerted her. But why? A woman who looked like her was surely accustomed to male attention.

Indeed, looking around now, he noticed a number of men glancing her way, a fact that tightened his jaw, and he wondered, as he had that first night in her bedchamber, if she had a lover. If she didn't, it was obviously because she chose not to. Because he couldn't imagine any man with a pulse not wanting her.

Not that it mattered. Of course not. Still, he didn't like unanswered questions. Or this unwanted preoccupation with her. The fact that he had to keep reminding himself that she was more than she seemed, more than a simple widow living a quiet existence, that she had secrets—one or more of which could cost him his life— unsettled and confused him. He needed to keep his mind on his mission, and recall that Genevieve Ralston was merely a means to an end.

Keeping that in mind, he crossed the square, weaving his way toward her through the milling crowd. As he drew near, Baxter caught sight of him and sizzled a glare in his direction surely meant to reduce him to ashes.

"There you are, Mrs. Ralston," Simon said with a smile, offering her a formal bow. "Please forgive my tardiness. I was waylaid by half a dozen merchants and then couldn't locate you in this crowd. I had no idea so many people resided in Little Longstone."

"The festival draws visitors from miles around," she said, raising a gloved hand to shield her eyes from the sun. "I thought perhaps you'd decided against coming."

"Not at all." He looked into her clear blue eyes and experienced that same visceral punch of lust. Bloody hell, she looked like a succulent peach—ripe, delicious and ready to be plucked. Before he could stop himself, he stepped closer to her. The subtle scent of roses tickled his senses and he was struck by an overwhelming desire to press his face against her neck and breathe her in, then drag her off to the nearest deserted corner and strip her bare to discover if she smelled so delicious everywhere. "I've been looking forward to seeing you again," he said quietly. It wasn't until he spoke the words out loud that he realized just how true they were.

Her breath caught and her pupils dilated. The insane thought that thank God it wasn't just him experiencing this profound physical attraction ran through his mind. For several seconds he felt as if he were under some sort of spell, trapped by her gaze and the desire he saw simmering there. It was as if everything faded away except her. The noise, the crowd, the music, all seemed to evaporate, leaving just the two of them. Her lips parted slightly, drawing his attention to her mouth. Her lush, delicious mouth that beckoned him like a siren's call. In his mind's eye he saw himself leaning forward... brushing his lips over hers—

"Saw a number of folks with pups fer sale." Baxter's gruff voice broke through the fog surrounding Simon and he turned toward the giant man. And found himself the recipient of another dark scowl. "Can't say how many beasts might be left, seein' as how ye saw fit to turn up an hour late." Baxter narrowed his eyes. "I didn't see ye talkin' with any merchants."

"Nor did I see you," Simon said smoothly. "Or any dogs for sale. Where are they?"

Baxter jerked his thumb over his shoulder. "Back that way. I'll show ye."

Baxter managed to make *I'll show ye* sound like *I'll pulverize yer bones then toss ye into the Thames*. Before Simon could reply, Mrs. Ralston said, "I'll show Mr. Cooper the pups, Baxter."

Baxter clearly planned to veto that suggestion, but once again, Mrs. Ralston spoke, this time in an undertone. "Miss Mary Winslow is headed this way—" she glanced over Baxter's broad shoulder "—looking very much in need of an escort."

Baxter turned his head so fast Simon swore he heard the man's neck snap. Simon shifted and watched a pretty young woman with dark-red hair and light-brown eyes approach. "Good afternoon, Baxter," she said with a shy, dimpling smile, stopping next to him.

To Simon's utter amazement, a deep scarlet flush suffused the bald man's cheeks. "Uh, I…I… Good afternoon, Miss Winslow."

"And to you, too, Mrs. Ralston. Lovely day, isn't it?"

"Indeed it is," Mrs. Ralston answered. Although her expression was suitably serious, Simon could hear the whiff of amusement in her voice. "Have you met Mr. Cooper? He has let Dr. Oliver's cottage for the next two weeks."

Simon made a formal bow, relieved that Mrs. Ralston had undertaken the introductions. In his amazement over Baxter's reaction to the young woman, Simon might well have momentarily forgotten that here in Little Longstone he was Mr. Simon Cooper, not Simon Cooperstone, Viscount Kilburn. "A pleasure, Miss Winslow."

Miss Winslow inclined her head. "Mr. Cooper. Welcome to Little Longstone." She offered him a bright smile. "Heavens, we've all sorts of newcomers. First that artist fellow, Mr. Blackwell, and now Mr. Cooper. I hope you enjoy your stay."

"I'm certain I will, thank you."

Miss Winslow returned her attention to Baxter who seemed nailed in place, gazing upon her with such an utterly besotted expression Simon had to bite the insides of his cheeks to keep from laughing. When the giant remained mute, Mrs. Ralston suggested gently, "Perhaps Miss Winslow would enjoy a meat pie, Baxter."

"Oh, yes, I would," replied Miss Winslow, nodding.

Baxter swallowed hard. "I…I… Meat pie. Yes. Good." Then he seemed to recall himself and managed to tear his gaze away from Miss Winslow long enough to give Simon another fulminating glare. "I'll be close by should ye need me," he said to Mrs. Ralston before extending a beefy arm to the petite Miss Winslow.

After they'd drifted off into the crowd, Simon turned to Mrs. Ralston, who still stared after the departing couple. "Baxter may be hewn of granite on the outside, but on the inside he's—"

"Overcooked porridge," Mrs. Ralston said, turning toward him. A slow smile curved her lips. "Please don't let on that you know."

"His secret is safe with me. I must say, I don't believe I've ever before seen anyone manage to appear flushed and pale at the same time."

Mrs. Ralston laughed. "Yes, that's quite a feat."

"Clearly that little devil Cupid shot an entire quiver of arrows at Baxter."

"Indeed," Mrs. Ralston agreed. "I've known Baxter for more than half my life and I've never seen him so smitten." She pursed her lips and gave him an arch look. "Perhaps when you see the puppies offered today you'll find yourself equally besotted, Mr. Cooper."

Staring into her beautiful blue eyes, Simon's heart began to pound with hard, erratic beats and he indeed found himself feeling besotted. Ridiculously so. Annoyingly so. Unacceptably so. It was one thing to seduce the woman to glean the information he needed. It was quite another to fall victim to her obviously potent charms. That was a trap he had no intention of falling into.

"Perhaps," he said. He extended his hand in the direction Baxter had indicated. "Shall we go see?"

6

"I DON'T BELIEVE I've ever seen anyone fall in love quite so quickly," Genevieve remarked an hour later as she and Mr. Cooper slowly made their way through the noisy hustle and bustle of the festival. She eyed the tail-wagging puppy secured in the curve of Mr. Cooper's arm. The bright-eyed dog eagerly looked about for something to lick with her active pink tongue.

Mr. Cooper's lips curved upward and Genevieve's breath caught. Dear God, that slow, lopsided smile of his was simply dazzling. "She *was* rather taken with me, wasn't she?" There was no missing the smug, male satisfaction in his voice.

Genevieve hiked up a single brow. "Yes. However, I meant *you* falling in love with *her*. You dropped like a brick tossed in the Thames."

"Clearly I harbor a weakness for pale-haired beauties," he murmured, his green eyes resting on hers while his long fingers ruffled the puppy's fur.

Genevieve's midsection tightened and she pulled in a slow breath, mentally chiding herself for her reaction. She didn't want to feel this heightened sense of awareness. This giddy sensation that threatened to bubble up and burst forth like the air in the hot springs. His every look, every brush of his shoulders against hers, shot heat through her, warmth that settled low in her belly and couldn't be called anything other than what it was—desire.

She tried to ignore it, but failed completely. Her common sense chided her that it was ridiculous and unseemly. Yet it was apparently unstoppable.

Clearing her throat, she said, "You also clearly harbor a weakness for rambunctious dogs. You realize she was the naughtiest pup in the entire litter."

"I noticed. However, I like naughty."

Another layer of heat engulfed her. "Perhaps that's what you should name her—Naughty."

"That's certainly better than what her previous owners called her." He held the puppy out at arm's length. "You didn't like being called Daffodil, did you?"

The puppy yipped twice in apparent agreement and wriggled to lick Mr. Cooper's wrist. "Of course you didn't," he said, pulling the dog against his broad chest. Genevieve noticed the energetic animal immediately quieted—except for its tongue which enthusiastically bathed the underside of Mr. Cooper's jaw.

Unable to help herself, Genevieve laughed. "I don't believe I've ever seen a dog more determined to kiss anyone."

"How fortunate that I harbor a weakness for kisses as well."

Her gaze snapped up from the dog to his eyes and found him regarding her with unmistakable heat. "Perhaps you should name her Licker." Heavens, was that breathless sound her voice?

"Perhaps. After all, there's much to be said for a well-placed lick."

An image immediately rose in Genevieve's mind... of his tongue brushing across her bottom lip. Then trailing down her throat. Between her breasts. Then lazily circling her nipple—

"But as you helped me choose her, I thought I'd name her after you," he continued, jerking her from her errant thoughts.

She had to swallow to locate her voice. "You wish to name your dog Genevieve?"

"A lovely name. But as it's already taken, I thought I'd name her Beauty."

Genevieve blinked. Pleasure washed through her, and, to her dismay she found herself utterly charmed. Surely she never used to fall victim to meaningless flattery so easily? Had she? She couldn't recall. Most likely because it had been so long since any man had flattered her. Had found her attractive. Had made her feel desire. And desirable. And as much as she might wish it otherwise, she found this man's attentions exhilarating. After Richard's rejection, she'd forced herself to forget how this wanting, this physical need had felt, but now…now it was all rushing back, so quickly it was as if she were drowning.

Yet she needed to recall that she didn't know this man. And even if she did, it wouldn't matter. She pressed her gloved hands together, wincing at the soreness in her joints. She wouldn't, couldn't allow things between them to advance beyond a mild flirtation under any circumstances. She had no reason to trust him. Indeed, she had more reason to be suspicious of him and of his motives for coming to Little Longstone, for seeking her out. And for borrowing her copy of the *Ladies' Guide.* Was he on a simple holiday as he'd claimed—or on a mission to discover Charles Brightmore's whereabouts? Why had he chosen that particular book? It was a question she needed answered. Now.

He wished to flirt? Fine. She wanted to learn his true motives and had no qualms about playing the coquette to find out what she wished to know.

"Beauty is a lovely name," she said, "but I suspect Devil might be more apt."

"Perhaps, but I like challenges."

She slanted him a sideways glance. "Is that why you borrowed *A Ladies' Guide to the Pursuit of Personal Happiness and Intimate Fulfillment* from me? Because you thought reading such a book would present a challenge?"

She watched him carefully, looking for any sign of guilt, but couldn't detect anything other than a slight sheepishness in his expression. He flashed her one of his disarming smiles. "I suppose it must seem an odd choice, but the title captured my attention."

"Why? Are you normally in the habit of reading ladies' guides?"

He gave a light laugh. "No. I hope you don't mind that I chose to borrow it?"

"No. Merely curious as to why you would."

"The title struck a chord in my memory. I recalled that there was some scandal attached to the book and its author, so I thought it might be an interesting read. Certainly a departure for me. And I was right."

Her brows shot up. "You've already read it?"

He nodded. "Last night."

When he offered nothing further, she couldn't help but ask, "And what did you think of it?"

"Given the explicit nature of the content, I can see why it caused a scandal. I also think Charles Brightmore knows more about women than any man I've ever met. Clearly the book required a great deal of research on his part." A whiff of mischief gleamed in his eyes. "He's a lucky man."

"And an exiled man." she said lightly, watching his reaction. "He left England after threats were made against him."

He frowned then nodded. "Yes, now that you mention it, I recall hearing that as well. Shame. Personally, I think he should be awarded a trophy."

"Oh? Why is that?"

"Because his book provides information not readily available anywhere else. I believe knowledge equates to power."

She couldn't hide her surprise. "Yet that was what those who made threats against him objected to. They didn't want women to have such information, or anything for that matter, that might equate to power."

"Then I can only say that those people are ignorant. Personally, I prefer well-informed, intelligent women." His intense green gaze roamed her face. "Indeed, you might say I harbor a weakness for them."

She ignored the warmth spreading through her at his unabashedly admiring regard. "You're apparently a man of many weaknesses, Mr. Cooper."

For several seconds he said nothing, just looked at her with an expression she couldn't decipher other than to know it made her skin feel as if it were on fire. Finally he cleared his throat then said softly, "So it seems."

She moistened her suddenly dust-dry lips, noting how his gaze dropped to her mouth. "So…you've no objection to women having information, even if that knowledge might lead to power?"

"Knowledge, experience, power…I find them all very attractive qualities in a woman." His gaze again flicked to her lips. "Very attractive."

"You're not afraid of being…overpowered?"

His gaze caught fire and seemed to burn into hers. "I suppose that would depend on who was doing the overpowering."

The certainty that his meaning encompassed more than knowledge rippled a secret thrill through Genevieve, one that set up an insistent throb between her thighs. She'd led the conversation into these treacherous waters to determine if he had any interest in her connection to Charles Brightmore, and, unless he was a superb actor, it appeared he didn't. That was good, and a huge relief to be sure. The way he made her feel, however—as if her clothes were suddenly too tight and her skin too small—was not good. It was, in fact, most alarming.

Yet, she couldn't seem to stop herself from wading further into the hot, churning waters he inspired. Wasn't there a saying about keeping one's friends close but one's enemies closer? Perhaps Mr. Cooper wasn't her enemy, but neither could she call him a friend. Besides, what harm could there be in a little flirting? He wasn't a titled gentleman looking for a mistress, merely a steward enjoying a brief holiday. They were surrounded by hundreds of people. Nothing could or would come of it. She'd see to that. Indeed, given how he unsettled her, she had no intention of seeing him again after today. So surely there was no reason to deny herself the pleasure of indulging in a little fantasy…to pretend that she didn't have any physical flaws that would lead to rejection. To feel that she was free to touch and be touched, and to once again simply enjoy the company and admiration of a handsome young man. She could imagine herself…overpowering him. And him retaliating.

A delicious shiver trembled down her spine. She allowed her gaze to drift slowly over him, taking in the breadth of his shoulders, his strong hands holding his now-sleeping dog, the way his snug breeches clung to his muscular thighs, the play of those muscles with every step he took. When she once again met his gaze, she could tell he knew he'd just been ogled. And that he hadn't minded one bit. "How would someone go about overpowering a man like you, Mr. Cooper?"

"A man like me?"

"Strong. Capable." *Beautiful. Delicious. Physically perfect.*

"I suppose it would depend on who was doing the overpowering. Were you referring to someone specific? Such as yourself, perhaps?"

Genevieve's blood whooshed through her veins. "And if I were? Would I require a pistol or saber?"

Amusement kindled in his gaze. "Do you *have* a pistol and a saber?"

"Naturally. A woman needs protection, you know."

"I rather thought that's what Baxter was for."

"He certainly deters unwanted attention."

"When he's not baking scones."

Genevieve laughed. "Precisely."

"Well, in your case, neither a pistol nor a saber would be necessary. Beautiful women have been overpowering strong men for centuries with nothing more than a single touch."

Genevieve's fingers curled inside her gloves and she winced at the aching soreness in her joints. *A single touch...* Yes, at one time she'd been capable of overpowering, seducing a man with her touch. Before the arthritis had stricken her hands—slowly at first, just a few twinges, that had increased in frequency, intensity and duration. The combination of the hot springs and her cream had offered relief and had enabled her to hide her growing discomfort from Richard for months. But when the swelling had begun, she couldn't hide any longer.

She missed the woman she used be. Yet, since there was no point in dwelling on the past or on things she couldn't change, she opened her mouth to steer the subject into safer waters. Before she could, however, he added softly, "Of course, if a touch doesn't quite do the trick, there are other ways."

"Indeed? And what are those?"

"I'm surprised that a woman familiar with Bright- more's *Ladies' Guide* needs to ask."

At his mention of the *Guide,* her breath caught. She knew, of course, what he referred to. "Unlike you, I read it months ago. I fear my memory isn't as fresh as yours."

"Ah. Then allow me to remind you. According to Brightmore, Today's Modern Woman should not hesitate to insist upon getting what she wants, be it in the drawing room or in the bedchamber—even if she has to tie up her man to get it."

Genevieve's heart began to beat in slow, hard thuds. She'd written those words—or rather, dictated them to Catherine because Genevieve's hands had rendered writing so uncomfortable—never dreaming she'd hear a man recite them back to her. And so exactly. Clearly that passage had left an impression. "So you believe that a woman can overpower a man with ropes?"

"Not unless he's willing. As for ropes…" He shook his head. "Something softer, such as a satin ribbon, would be much more…pleasurable."

His quiet, husky tone dared her to contradict him. Which she needed to, of course. They were in a public place. Anyone might overhear them. Certainly anyone observing them would see the way he was looking at her. As if he wanted to devour her. And this conversation...it was completely improper. Beyond the pale. She needed to end this. Now.

Yet when she parted her lips, no words came forth. Nor could she pull her gaze away from his.

"Of course, if the lady wasn't quick to do the overpowering, she might find herself overpowered instead," he murmured.

An image of herself sprawled in her bed, her wrists bound with satin ribbons and him looming over her flashed through her mind.

Desire gushed through her, hardening her nipples, swelling the aching folds between her thighs, dampening her drawers. She felt flushed and out of breath and, damnation, she needed to sit down before her shaky knees gave away the fact that she felt less than steady.

As if he read her mind, he pointed to a copse of trees ahead, on the fringe of the festivities. "There's a bench over there. Would you like to sit down?"

Not trusting her voice, she nodded and quickened her pace, resolved that she'd sit only as long as she needed to to regain her composure, then she'd plead a headache and beg off from his company. Clearly, her instincts that had warned her there was more to his trip to Little Longstone than he'd told her had been wrong. She now felt fairly confident his reasons for being here had nothing to do with Charles Brightmore. Which meant they had nothing to do with her. Which meant there was no reason to prolong their outing or to see him again. She would return to her cottage, resume her routine of visiting the springs to ease the pain in her hands, and forget all about Simon Cooper.

Unfortunately, a little voice inside her whispered that forgetting about this man who had reawakened wants and needs she'd thought long buried would prove very challenging indeed.

7

"SO TELL ME, Mrs. Ralston, what else do you enjoying
doing aside from reading and indulging your weakness
for artwork?"

The instant they were seated on the wooden bench,
Simon tossed out the question as a matter of self-pres-
ervation. He'd suggested they sit because the sensual
waters their conversation had drifted into had made it
difficult for him to walk without limping. The image
that had haunted him since watching her in her bedchamber, of her tying his hands with her satin hair
ribbons, had roared into his mind, resulting in yet
another Genevieve Ralston-inspired arousal. Bloody
hell, he hadn't suffered so many unwanted erections
since he was a green lad.

No doubt part of the problem was the fact that he
hadn't been with a woman for several months, a situation that confounded him, since he'd had ample opportunity to end his celibacy at a number of soirées.
However, none of the ladies, in spite of their willingness
and beauty, had lit more than a superficial spark within
him. He wasn't quite certain when his liking for purely
physical, emotionally meaningless liaisons had waned,
but there was no denying that over the past year or so it
had. Until, it seems, he'd set eyes on Genevieve Ralston.

One look at her in that damn soaked chemise, and a purely physical, emotionally meaningless liaison was all he *could* think about.

He shifted his sleeping puppy more comfortably into the crook of his arm, and in spite of himself his lips twitched. He hadn't really been looking to purchase a dog, but as it had provided a perfect pretext to entice Mrs. Ralston into meeting him at the festival, he'd seized the opportunity. Otherwise, he feared, she might have refused his invitation, even though he sensed she found him attractive. Or perhaps she didn't. Unlike most women, he found her frustratingly difficult to read.

"I enjoy spending time in my garden," she answered.

Relief rushed through him. The garden. Excellent. Nothing sensual about that. "I saw something of it when I walked to your home yesterday. The grounds are lovely."

"Thank you. I find it very peaceful."

"And so well-tended. Perhaps you'd share the name of your gardener so I could pass it along to Dr. Oliver? I'm afraid his shrubs have become overgrown since he left Little Longstone."

"I'm actually in need of a new gardener myself. My dear friend Catherine used to help me—we'd spend hours together in the garden, but she recently married and now lives in London. Baxter's taken care of things since she left, but I'm afraid he has trouble telling the difference between what is and isn't a weed. And given his tendency to stomp about…" She chuckled. "I think he's scared several plants to death."

Simon nodded. "Gardening requires a delicate touch."

Her eyes took on a wistful expression. "Yes. I used to do it all myself…" Her gaze drifted down to her gloved hands which she'd hidden among the folds of her pelisse. "But as the garden grew, it became more than I could handle alone."

He followed her gaze. He noted she kept her hands out of sight as much possible, even though she wore gloves. She'd even worn them in her house during his visit yesterday, an oddity to be sure. He recalled how pained she'd looked when she'd been writing, the cream she'd rubbed into her hands in her bedchamber before donning her gloves to sleep, and her mention of the therapeutic springs. Clearly she'd suffered some sort of accident or injury. Curiosity jabbed him, but he pushed it away. If he pushed for too much information too soon, he feared scaring her off, and he couldn't risk that before he had his letter. Still, he needed to know more about her, needed to establish a connection between them. A connection of trust.

Before he could proceed, however, a young boy Simon judged to be perhaps eight, approached him, his round-eyed gaze fixed on Beauty.

"That's a fine puppy, sir," the lad said, drawing nearer. "May I pet him?"

"He's a she," Simon said with a smile. "And yes you may. But I warn you, if she wakes up, she'll want to slather you with doggie kisses."

The boy smiled, revealing a gap-toothed grin. "That's all right, sir. I like doggie kisses." He reached out and ran a slightly grubby hand over the dog's soft fur. "What's her name?"

"Beauty."

The boy's grin deepened. "And she's sleeping—just like the fairy tale." His expression turned serious. "'Cept she's a dog, not a princess. And I ain't a prince."

"Perhaps once she kisses you, you'll turn into one," Simon said.

The boy chuckled. "Doubt it. I'm going to be a sailor. Like my da."

Simon nodded gravely. "Excellent. England needs good sailors. And what is your name?"

"Benjamin Paxton, sir." The boy thrust out his none-too-clean hand.

Simon shook it. "Simon Cooper. And my friend, Mrs. Ralston, who helped me pick out Beauty."

Benjamin nodded at Mrs. Ralston. "A fine job you did. Got her from the blacksmith's litter, did you? I saw he was selling pups."

"Yes," Mrs. Ralston said. "Are you going to buy one?"

The boy scuffed the toe of his boot on the ground and shook his head. "We can't have a dog. They make my little sister sneeze and cough something awful." He ran his fingers over Beauty's fur. "Dogs don't make *me* cough and sneeze, though."

"Perhaps not," Simon said, "but it is a brother's duty to look after and protect his sister. I'd wager you're a very fine one."

Benjamin drew himself up then nodded. "Yes, sir. Rufus Templeton said mean things to Annabelle and I bloodied his nose for him."

"Good man. I've bloodied a few noses myself to defend my younger sister."

"It's what we men must do," Benjamin said gravely.

Just then Beauty awoke, and, as predicted, immediately looked for something to lick. Benjamin's fingers provided fertile ground.

"Would you like to hold her?" Simon asked.

Benjamin's eyes widened. "Oh, yes, sir."

Simon transferred the squirming bundle to the boy who dissolved into giggles when Beauty's busy tongue laved his chin. Simon couldn't help but chuckle and when he glanced at Mrs. Ralston, he noted her broad smile.

"She's certainly energetic," Benjamin managed to say between bouts of laughter.

"Yes. I think she needs a good run and I'm rather tired. Are you up for the task?"

"Yes, sir." Benjamin carefully set Beauty on the ground and fisted his hand around her lead. "I'll be very careful with her."

"I'm sure you will be." Simon pointed to the large clock mounted to the church tower on the opposite side of the square. "Why don't you bring her back here in about a quarter hour's time?"

"I'll do that, Mr. Cooper, and thank you, sir!" Benjamin trotted off, an eager Beauty prancing at his heels.

"I stand corrected," Mrs. Ralston said.

Simon turned and found her looking at him through amused eyes. "Regarding what?"

"I'd said I'd never seen anyone fall in love quite so quickly as you did with Beauty…and then little Benjamin came along and proved me wrong." Her low, husky laugh made Simon wonder if she'd make that same delightful sound in bed. "Asking that boy if he wanted to hold her was rather like me asking Sophia if she'd care for a rasher of fish."

"I take it Sophia likes fish?"

"It's merely her most favorite thing in the world."

Simon shook his head. "I'd wager *you* are her favorite thing in the world."

"Only because I am the one responsible for providing her with fish. As far as Sophia is concerned, the cottage belongs to her. I may remain as her guest only so long as I cater to her every need."

"I see. And if you don't?"

She heaved a dramatic sigh. "I fear I'd be cast aside with nary a thought."

"I disagree." Before he could stop himself, Simon gave in to temptation and propped his elbow on the back of the bench, allowing his fingertips to lightly graze her shoulder. Heat sizzled up his arm, a ridiculous reaction to such a whisper of a touch—to her *clothing*, no less. "It would be impossible to cast you aside."

She froze and Simon stilled as well at the unmistakable pain that flashed in her eyes. Clearly someone *had* cast this woman aside, someone she'd cared for deeply, and Simon's guess was Ridgemoor. Earlier, he'd wondered if, in spite of the information he'd gleaned that Ridgemoor had ended their affair, if perhaps their arrangement had ended at Mrs. Ralston's behest. But based on that look in her eyes, he doubted it. And he once again questioned how Ridgemoor could have tired of such an exquisite, intelligent, witty woman. Perhaps like many men, the earl had decided he preferred a woman who didn't present any intellectual challenge. Or perhaps Ridgemoor had suspected his paramour had secrets? Had those secrets cost the man his life?

"I've learned that nothing is impossible, Mr. Cooper," she murmured.

"Please, call me Simon. All my friends do."

She shifted, moving so his fingers no longer touched her, and lifted her chin. For the first time he noticed the tiny flecks of gold in her blue irises. Her eyes reminded him of a sun-dappled sea. And bloody hell if he didn't feel as if he were drowning.

"You consider us friends?" she asked.

"I'd like to. Certainly I consider you a friend to me. After all, you helped me choose my dog."

"You and Beauty chose each other without any assistance from me."

"Yet I wouldn't have known where to find her if not for you. Besides, you are the only person I know in Little Longstone." He dropped his chin and sent her an exaggerated woebegone look.

A whiff of amusement ghosted over her features. "Heavens, that is the saddest face I've ever seen. Do you practice that look in front of your mirror?"

"As a matter of fact, I do. Is it working?"

"Not a bit. I'm made of much sterner stuff than to fall victim to—"

"The saddest face you've ever seen?" he broke in, attempting to make his expression sadder still.

"Correct. And I'm not the only person you know in Little Longstone. You know Baxter."

"Yes. And if glares were knives, I'd have bled to death in your foyer yesterday, long before ever meeting you."

"And you know Benjamin."

"True." He arched a brow at her. "And I'm guessing that if I invited *him* to call me Simon, he'd accept—and ask me to call him by *his* given name."

She arched a brow right back at him. "I'm guessing that as Beauty's owner, you could have invited that child to call you Penelope and he would have obliged you."

Simon couldn't help but laugh. "You're no doubt correct. And he would have taken great joy in teasing me about it. He had a bit of mischief in his eye, that lad did. Reminds me of my nephew, Harry."

"How old is Harry?"

"Eight, although there are times I would swear he's eight and twenty."

"You mentioned a younger sister—is Harry her child?"

"Yes. Marjorie—my sister—also has a daughter. Lily is three, and if I may say so, the most beautiful child in the entire kingdom. When the time comes, her father is going to need a dozen brooms to sweep the suitors off his porch."

"Of course, you're not the least bit biased."

"Not the least bit," Simon agreed with a smile, his body relaxing a bit now that the conversation wasn't so steeped in sexual innuendo and he was no longer touching her.

"Do you have siblings other than Marjorie?"

"A younger brother. Robert's wife is expecting their first child this winter."

"You sound...wistful?"

Did he? Yes, he supposed he did. Robert and Beatrice had married ten months ago and were very much in love, a fact which pleased Simon for his brother's sake, but one that had left him examining his own life—and discovering that in spite of all his good fortune, his work for the Crown, he still felt unfulfilled. Which perhaps explained the discontent he'd been unable to shake the last few months.

"Perhaps a bit wistful," he conceded. "Both my siblings are very happy in their respective marriages. It sometimes makes me, well, envious, even while I'm delighted for them."

"Then perhaps you should marry."

"A fine idea, however, to the best of my knowledge, a wedding requires a bride as well as a groom," he said lightly while inwardly wincing. Bloody hell, what was

he saying? A fine idea? He'd managed to avoid the mat-
rimonial noose so far. Yet even as that thought crossed
his mind, he had to admit that lately the idea of taking
a wife didn't seem like such a rope around his neck.
Indeed, the thought of sharing his life with someone,
having the sort of relationship that Robert and Beatrice
enjoyed, that Marjorie and Charles shared, wasn't
entirely unpleasant.

Over the last year he'd grown increasingly tired of
transient lovers, of moving from one social rout to the
next. Much of his socializing in society's upper circles
was done purely for investigative purposes—to keep
his eyes and ears open. His society peers were ignorant
of his connection to the Crown, which enabled Simon
to gather very useful information. But the constant
demands on him had become wearying, and lately he
had found himself longing to just…be. To be able to
enjoy his country estate rather than be forced to remain
in London or travel to the continent for missions. Not
to have to constantly lie to his friends and family about
his doings. Not to have to look over his shoulder for
danger. Not to have to prove to his peers and superiors
that he was innocent of murder…

While he was proud of the work he'd done for the
Crown, of what he'd accomplished, the traitors he'd
brought to justice, there was no denying the sense that
something was missing from his life.

"Have you *looked* for a bride?" she asked.

Her question jerked him from his brown study.
Looked for a bride? God, no. Indeed, he'd had to
perform some very fancy sidestepping from matchmak-
ing mamas over the years to avoid having one. A fact
which suddenly didn't please him as much as it should

have. "I'm afraid I've yet to find anyone who's inspired me to propose."

"Come, come now, Mr. Cooper. I'm certain there's a trail of broken hearts behind you."

He almost laughed out loud. To the best of his knowledge, none of his former lovers' hearts had been involved in their brief trysts. Certainly his heart hadn't been. "Not that I'm aware of. Why do think that?"

Her brows rose. "On the basis of your looks alone, I'm certain you don't lack for attention."

"I could say the same to you."

"I'm not looking for attention."

"You think I am?"

"Aren't all men?"

He laughed. "So…you think me handsome?" he asked in a teasing tone.

She laughed. "Heavens, I've never known anyone to fish for compliments with less subtlety."

"I was merely making certain I understood your meaning."

"You understood perfectly."

"In that case, thank you. And allow me to return the compliment. You are—" his gaze wandered over her and all the relaxation he'd briefly achieved vanished in what felt like an engulfment of steam; he raised his gaze back to hers and once again he felt himself drowning in those eyes "—exquisite."

His words, or perhaps his obvious desire, or perhaps both, clearly flustered her. Instead of acknowledging either, she said, "I can only conclude that the reason you don't have a wife is because you haven't wanted one."

Which was absolutely true. Yet, hearing her say it unreasonably irked him. "Perhaps it's because I haven't fallen in love." That was certainly true—he never had. And even though he'd never allowed himself to become emotionally entangled due to the secretive nature of his spy work for the Crown, he suddenly realized he hadn't had to put forth much effort to avoid it. He'd yet to meet a woman who affected him in more than a superficial, fleeting way.

She studied him for several seconds, her clear blue eyes searching his, and he wished he knew what she was thinking. Finally she asked, "You've never been in love?"

"No. Have you?"

Her expression turned cool. "You ask this of a woman who was married?"

"I meant no offense. But you cannot deny that not all marriages are based on love."

"No, I suppose they're not."

"What was your husband's name?"

She hesitated, then said softly, "Richard."

Her answer was precisely what he had suspected she'd say. Richard was Lord Ridgemoor's Christian name. Simon was beginning to believe that there never had been a Mr. Ralston. Only her lover, Ridgemoor, whom she had clearly loved. And who, based on her reactions, had cast her aside. Did she have any idea that her former lover was dead? Certainly she would know if she was in any way involved in his death.

"You loved him very much." It wasn't a question.

She pulled her gaze from his and looked down at her lap, but not before he detected the sheen of tears in her eyes. Tears of sorrow for losing the man she loved—or tears of guilt, for complicity in his death?

"Yes," she whispered. "I loved him."

The heartfelt sincerity in her words, her tone, unexpectedly touched Simon in a way he didn't quite understand. Reaching out, he gently laid one of his hands on her tightly clasped ones. "I'm sorry."

She went perfectly still for several seconds. Then a shudder seemed to rack her entire body. She snatched her hands from beneath his and abruptly stood. "I must go," she said, her voice agitated.

Simon rose. "Are you all right?" he asked. Ridiculous question. It was obvious something was amiss, yet he didn't know what else to say.

"I'm fine. I simply recalled a previous engagement, one to which I'm already late. Thank you for the outing. Good day, Mr. Cooper." With that she turned and strode quickly away from him.

Simon's first impulse was to go after her, but he forced himself not to. Instead he watched her melt into the crowd.

He didn't believe for a minute that there was a previous engagement, so what had sent her fleeing from him? Grief? Or perhaps guilt over her lost love? Or was it his touch that had sent her away? His guess was the latter, which then begged the question why. That gentle touch couldn't have hurt her, yet she'd fled as if he'd burned her. Had that brief connection affected her the same way it had him—filling him with a deep hunger for more? Or was it aversion that had her running away? She clearly shied away from touching, no doubt because of whatever the problem was with her hands.

Simon blew out a sigh and slowly sat back down to await Benjamin's return with Beauty. Genevieve Ralston inspired far too many questions—questions that would be damned difficult to answer under the best of circumstances. To make matters worse, the lady wasn't being honest with him. Certainly she hadn't been forthcoming about her past, although he couldn't blame her for not telling him she'd spent ten years as a nobleman's mistress. Or that she'd authored the most scandalous book of the decade.

Nor could he throw any stones, given the glass house in which he dwelled. He certainly hadn't been honest with her about who he was or why he was in Little Longstone. Given his suspicions regarding her and the number of lies he'd been forced to tell over the years, this shouldn't have bothered him. Yet it did.

He heaved a weary sigh. He needed to bury his conscience and concentrate on finding that damn letter, getting it back to London and into Waverly's hands, so that together they could clear Simon's name.

Still…how would it feel to tell someone the unvarnished truth? A humorless sound escaped him. It had been so long since he'd done so, he couldn't recall. But he imagined it would be…liberating.

Of course he couldn't, wouldn't consider saying or doing anything that could jeopardize his mission. Still, he idly wondered what her reaction would be if he were honest with her. What if he told her he was a spy for the Crown? That his true surname was Cooperstone? And that he wasn't a steward but a viscount? The spy revelation would no doubt shock her, as it would his acquaintances, friends and family. Very few people knew about his secret life. As for his exalted title—would he see the same flicker of greed he observed in so many other women's eyes? That glimmer of assessment as they calculated how much they could get from him? A bracelet? A necklace? A proposal?

Before he could ponder the question further, an odd chill stole over him—a sensation he well recognized after spending eight years in the spy game.

He was being watched.

He scanned the crowd, but saw nothing amiss. No one's attention appeared fixed on him. Keeping his movements casual, he rose and glanced around. Hundreds of people milled about, none of whom he recognized, none of whom seemed the least interested in him. Yet he felt the weight of someone's eyes on him. And he sensed danger.

No one except his butler knew he was here, and he'd sworn Ramsey to secrecy. He looked around again, but the feeling of danger faded, convincing him that whoever had been watching him was no longer nearby. Every instinct screamed that whoever it was had to be connected to the letter he sought, which made Simon's mission even more urgent. He needed to find that letter—before someone else did.

8

GENEVIEVE paced the length of her bedchamber, pausing at the window to stare down at her garden. Moonlight bathed the gravel paths winding between the hedges and plants. Usually the sight calmed her, but not tonight. Her thoughts had been in turmoil ever since she'd walked away from Mr. Cooper this afternoon after they'd chatted and laughed together, after he'd flirted with her, and she'd flirted back.

After he'd touched her.

Genevieve closed her eyes and rested her forehead against the cool glass, recalling the unforgettable sensation of his fingertips brushing over her shoulder. So light a caress to inspire such heat within her. She should have left then. But she'd been enjoying his company and the admiration and want in his eyes. It had been so long since she'd been desired, felt desirable. It had been so long since she'd experienced the longing tug, the yearning of sensual need. So, instead of listening to her better judgment, she'd simply shifted away from his touch and stayed, basking in his attention.

But then he'd laid his hand over hers, and she'd frozen, shocked by the unexpected touch. No one had touched her hands in a year. Fear had momentarily paralyzed her. Could he feel the swollen joints beneath her gloves? Did he know the ugliness that marred her? Would the disfigurement that had caused Richard to reject her affect him similarly? The warmth of his hand over hers penetrated the soft leather, melting her fear with a fire that seemed to engulf her, filling her with the overwhelming need to touch him in return, feel his hands on her, and hers on him. Those unwanted, dangerous needs would ultimately only lead to hurt and rejection. And she'd had enough of those to last a lifetime.

But then why, *why* couldn't she banish this man from her thoughts? Why could she not rid her mind of the unwanted fantasies he inspired? She pictured herself coming naked to his bed…of having him naked in hers. Kissing, touching, exploring—her hands were perfect as they glided over his body. She should be sleeping in her own bed right now, not pacing the floor with her skin on fire and her heart beating in rapid, hard punches against her ribs. She pressed her thighs together to relieve the insistent ache between her legs, but the friction only served to frustrate her further.

There was only one way to relieve the tension gripping her—a soak in the hot springs. She lifted her head and glanced at the mantel clock. It was just after midnight, but that didn't matter. She often visited the springs late at night, when the pain in her hands prevented her from sleeping. Tonight she suffered from a different sort of ache, one she hoped a good soaking would diminish.

She kicked off her slippers, replacing them with sturdier boots, then she grabbed the small pistol she kept hidden in her wardrobe. She'd never been threatened in any way, either by a person or an animal during her nocturnal visits to the springs, but better to be careful than sorry. She hurried down the stairs and pulled her cloak from the brass rack by the door. After donning the garment and slipping the pistol in the pocket, she silently left the house. Not that silence was needed. Baxter's quarters occupied the far corner of the cottage, and he always slept as if he'd been hit on the head with an anvil. Just as well; she knew he would strenuously object to her visiting the springs at night alone. Still, what he didn't know, he couldn't worry about.

The moon provided a bright, silvery light, but she could have navigated the familiar route through the thick copses of trees without it. She breathed in the cool, crisp air and immediately felt a layer of tension slide from her shoulders. After a brisk five-minute walk, she arrived. Surrounded on three sides by an outcropping of rocks that provided privacy, the circular spring wasn't large, no more than eight feet in diameter, the water only deep enough to reach her shoulders. A submerged natural ledge curved around a three-foot section close to the rocks, providing a perfect seat. Genevieve shed her gloves, cloak, robe and boots, leaving her clad only in a chemise. After setting her pistol within easy reach next to her bundle of clothing, she stepped down into the heated water.

She settled herself on the stone seat and breathed out a long, satisfied *aaaahhhh* as the bubbling warmth surrounded her. The heat brought instant relief to her hands which she slowly flexed, and after several minutes the tightness in her limbs gave way to a delicious languor. Her eyes slid closed and she concentrated on emptying her mind of everything save the soothing sensation of the water lapping around her. Unfortunately, images of exactly what she was desperately trying to forget rose in her mind's eye...Mr. Cooper. Joining her at the springs. His green eyes devouring her as he entered the water. His body pressed against hers, relieving all the throbbing aches he inspired.

With a groan, Genevieve spread her legs and pulled up her chemise to her waist. The bubbling water caressed her exposed, aroused sex, but it wasn't enough to alleviate her discomfort. She skimmed one hand over her stomach, between her thighs and separated her swollen folds, while her other hand cupped her breast. With a deep sigh, she imagined it was his hands bringing her pleasure, circling, fondling, tugging, rubbing, delving. A low moan escaped her and her head fell back. She spread her legs wider and raised her hips, desperately seeking the relief that remained just out of reach. She was a single breath away from her climax when she heard a loud crashing in the underbrush, followed by a string of curses uttered in a deep, masculine voice.

Her eyes popped open. She saw no one in the surrounding woods, but the voice was close by. Heart pounding, she reached for her pistol.

"Bloody hell, come back here." The man's call broke through the trees, followed by the blur of an animal. A heartbeat later a tall figure skidded to a stop at the small clearing containing the spring. Indeed, he halted barely before he would have fallen into the water.

"What the devil—"

Clearly the intruder saw her pistol because his words cut off and he slowly raised his hands. Genevieve looked up to where he stood illuminated in a streak of silvery moonlight and was about to inform him that she wouldn't hesitate to shoot him if he came any closer when recognition hit her.

"Mr. Cooper?"

Her relief that it wasn't some stranger or footpad was quickly tempered by the heat that flooded her. Dear God, she'd just been fantasizing about him, thoughts that had left her teetering on the brink of orgasm. Now here he stood, looking tall and strong and masculine, slightly disheveled and far too delicious by half.

At the sound of his name his gaze snapped up from the pistol to her face. And he blinked. "Mrs. Ralston. What are you doing here?"

Genevieve's brows shot upward. "I believe that's what I should ask you, seeing as you're trespassing on my property."

"And I'll be delighted to tell you—as soon as you put down your weapon. Unless you plan to shoot me?"

"You're fortunate I didn't."

Now his brows rose. "Do you know how to use that thing?"

She smiled sweetly. "Perfectly. Would you care for a demonstration?"

"Ah, no. Happy to take your word for it. Now if you wouldn't mind…" He gave the pistol a pointed look then jerked his head toward the rim of the spring.

"You seem a bit unsettled, Mr. Cooper."

"Do I? No doubt because I'm surprised. I wasn't anticipating having a pistol pointed at me." His gaze swept over her. "Or running across a wet, naked woman."

Heat that had nothing to do with the warm water rippled through Genevieve. Raising her chin she informed him, "I'm not naked."

"How…unfortunate." He gave the pistol another pointed stare. "I assure you that weapon isn't necessary."

She slowly set the pistol aside, fighting her reluctance

to do so. Even though she didn't believe he meant her any harm, releasing the cool metal rendered her vulnerable, especially given her lack of clothing and the fact that she was up to her shoulders in water.

After placing the weapon next to her pile of clothing, she quickly submerged her hands and glared up at him, anger replacing her surprise. "You nearly startled me out of my skin. What are you doing here?" She narrowed her eyes. "Are you spying on me?"

"No." His gaze skimmed over her, lingering for several seconds on the swell of her breasts visible above the bubbling water before returning to her eyes. "Although had I known I'd make such a delightful discovery, I would have—"

"*Spied* on me?" she asked in her most scathing voice.

"Arrived here sooner."

His quiet words hung in the air between them, momentarily stealing Genevieve's ability to speak. If he'd arrived any sooner, or with any sort of stealth, he would have seen her pleasuring herself. Her nipples hardened at the thought and she scooted down a bit lower.

"You still haven't explained your presence, Mr. Cooper." Botheration, instead of sounding annoyed, she sounded absolutely breathless.

"Beauty," he said, nodding toward the edge of the spring. Genevieve turned. His mischievous puppy stood next to her pile of clothing, tongue lolling, tail wagging. Upon hearing her name, Beauty barked twice.

"That beast has run me all over Little Longstone," Mr. Cooper said. "She managed to chew through her lead and led me on a merry chase that brought me here."

As he spoke, Beauty let out a huge yawn, circled

twice, then settled herself atop Genevieve's clothing and closed her eyes.

"Oh, that's rich," Mr. Cooper said, his voice half amused, half aggravated. "I've trotted over half the kingdom trying to catch up with that imp, and *now* she decides to take a nap." He shot the sleepy puppy an exasperated look. "Why couldn't you have decided to do this several miles ago?"

Genevieve pressed her lips together to suppress her amusement. "Exercise is good for both the body and the spirit, Mr. Cooper."

"Yes, in the morning or afternoon. Or even the early evening. At midnight, however, it is merely an aggravation." He scowled at his pet who'd already fallen asleep, then shifted his attention back to Genevieve. "Would you like a dog?"

She laughed at his disgruntled tone. "No, thank you. If I brought home a puppy, I'm certain Sophia would be most displeased."

"Would you like to trade pets?"

"I'm almost tempted to agree just to call your bluff. You adore that puppy and you know it."

"*Now* I do. She's an angel when she's sleeping."

"What happened to the man who enjoyed a challenge?"

"He's right here—out of breath from all the running he's done after that mischievous beast…and looking at you." He moved to the edge of the spring and crouched down, resting his forearms on his knees. "And what an exquisite view it is. Now it's your turn. What are you doing here?"

"Surely that is obvious. I'm taking the waters."

"At this time of night?" He looked around. "Alone?"

"I often take the waters at night. It helps me to sleep.

And I *was* alone—until you and Beauty crashed into the clearing."

He lowered one arm and dipped his fingertips into the water. "Baxter isn't nearby to protect you?"

"No."

"As protective as he is of you, I can only assume he doesn't know you're here."

"No, he doesn't. Not that it's any of his concern. Or yours. I have my pistol for protection. But this isn't London, Mr. Cooper. There aren't footpads lurking in the shadows. Indeed, this is the first time I've ever encountered anyone on one of my nocturnal visits."

"So you do this often—come here at night?"

She pulled her gaze away from the oddly arousing sight of his long fingers slowly circling the surface of the water and hiked up her chin another notch. "As a matter of fact I do, yes."

"And you came tonight because you couldn't sleep." His soft, husky words were a statement rather than a question.

"Yes. That and the fact that the weather is perfect for a brisk walk and a soak."

"Why couldn't you sleep?"

Because I couldn't stop thinking about you. Imagining you touching me. Kissing me. Making love to me. Because the desire I feel for you is so overwhelming, I can barely think properly. "No particular reason. I just have a great deal on my mind."

"Something we have in common. I couldn't sleep either. That is why I thought to take Beauty for a walk—to tire us both out."

She arched a glance toward the sleeping dog. "It worked very well for Beauty."

"Yes. Not so well for me."

Silence swelled between them. His eyes glittered and his hand kept drawing those slow, hypnotic circles in the water. Genevieve had to fight to keep her breathing slow and steady under his unwavering regard. Her better judgment coughed to life, demanding she tell him to leave. Immediately. But she couldn't seem to force the words from her suddenly dry throat. Indeed, all she could do was stare back at him. And wonder if he was experiencing this same stifling tension and profound attraction that was all but suffocating her.

His gaze flicked to his circling hand. "The water feels good. Warm."

She nodded and forced out the only word she could manage. "Yes."

His gaze burned into hers. "Aren't you going to ask me why I couldn't sleep?"

She had to swallow twice to locate her voice, and even then it only came out in a whisper. "Why couldn't you sleep?"

"Because of you." He sat down on the ledge and yanked off one of his low boots. "I couldn't stop thinking about you." He tossed the boot aside, peeled off his stocking, then applied himself to his other boot.

She gaped at his bare foot. She opened her mouth to speak—only to discover that her jaw was hanging open. "Wh-what are you doing?"

"Telling you why I couldn't sleep. Every time I closed my eyes, all I saw was your face. Your smile. Your eyes. Do you have any idea how extraordinary your eyes are?"

"No—"

"They're the most gorgeous shade of blue I've ever seen. Like a cloudless sky on a summer day. And those gold flecks in them…stunning. And so expressive." He tossed aside the second boot and stocking. "But they're not always. Sometimes they're frustratingly difficult to read—"

"No, I meant what are you doing with your boots."

"Oh. I'm removing them."

"Yes, I see that. But why?"

"They're old favorites and I'd prefer not to ruin them." He rose and shrugged his jacket from his shoulders. Then began untying his cravat.

"*Now* what are you doing?"

"Removing my cravat."

"Again, I must ask why."

"Because I cannot remove my shirt without doing so. You did say the water felt nice."

"It does, but…"

Her words died when he pulled his shirt from his snug breeches and yanked the garment over his head.

Oh, my. Simon Cooper might not like to exercise at midnight, but his body gave testament to the fact that he partook of physical activities at other times. Her stupefied gaze traveled over his broad chest, thick and well-defined with muscle and covered with a shading of crisp ebony hair that tapered into a thin ribbon and bisected his ridged abdomen, a fascinating trail that her avid gaze followed until it was obscured by the waistband of his breeches. The impressive bulge pressing against the front of the snug black material gave proof that she wasn't alone in her desires.

Before she could pull a breath into her stalled lungs, he moved to the edge of the spring.

"Wh-what are you doing now?"

He slipped into the water. "I'm joining you."

9

HIS WORDS sucked the oxygen from Genevieve's lungs. She stared transfixed as Mr. Cooper, with his gaze steady on hers and bubbles foaming around his ribcage, slowly swished his arms through the water. The play of muscles in his powerful shoulders flexed with the movement, lulling her into a trance, rendering her incapable of doing anything save stare. Surely she should say something, demand he stop, but the only words rushing into her throat were *Oh, my, you are magnificent.* Indeed, she had to press her lips together to prevent herself from saying them out loud.

"You're right," he said, his husky voice rippling a heated tremor through her. "It does feel good."

Oh. Dear. God. She pressed her spine against the rock ledge to hold herself upright lest she slither beneath the surface of the water from a combination of surprise, apprehension and desire so strong it threatened to choke her. She yanked herself from the stupor into which she'd fallen and lifted to chin. "That was merely a statement of fact, Mr. Cooper. Not an invitation."

"Wasn't it?" He moved slowly toward her and she shrank farther into the shadows. "I think it was. Because there's something between us. Something I've felt since the first moment I saw you. A desire so strong I can barely think properly."

His words, which so precisely mirrored her own thoughts just moments ago, halted her breath. All she could think was, *Thank God, it's not just me.*

He stopped directly in front of her, then braced his hands on the stone ledge on either side of her, caging her in. Mere inches separated their bodies, a distance that simultaneously felt far too close and not nearly close enough. Genevieve sent up a silent prayer of thanks for the darkness and shadows. Although she tried to arrange her features into a cool mask, she doubted her ability to fully hide her desire for him.

"Can you look me in the eyes and tell me you don't feel it, too?" His gaze searched hers. Looking into his compelling eyes she felt as if she were falling into an abyss.

Dear God, how could she deny it? She hadn't felt need this profound since…she couldn't recall. Had she ever? Heaven help her, she didn't know. Yet to admit it would set her on a course she wasn't prepared to take.

Or was she? It was dark…dark enough to hide her hands, and the water would do the same. He wouldn't be able to see them, wouldn't know…and therefore wouldn't have any reason to reject her.

Did she dare?

Before she could decide, he leaned forward until his lips hovered a mere hairbreadth above hers. His scent surrounded her, a delicious combination of soap, warm skin and a hint of sandalwood.

"Do you feel it?" he whispered. The words resembled a growl and blew warmth across her lips. "Bloody hell, say something. Tell me it's not just me who feels this."

A shudder of raw, naked wanting wracked her,

shaking her with its intensity, and all the reasons she should push him away faded into oblivion. "It's not just you," she whispered back.

"Thank God." The words sounded like a fervent prayer and in the next instant his arms were around her, hauling her up and against him. His mouth slanted over hers, and, with a moan, Genevieve parted her lips and welcomed the delicious invasion of his tongue. In a heartbeat she was lost, her senses reeling with long-forgotten sensations. He felt so incredibly good. Big and strong, hard and solid. And he tasted so wonderful—like mint with a hint of fine brandy. A groan vibrated in her throat at the erotic friction of his tongue exploring her mouth, of the press of his erection against her belly. She wrapped her arms around his neck and plunged impatient fingers through his thick, silky hair to drag his head closer.

Touch him…she wanted, needed to touch him. *Had* to touch him. She skimmed her hands across his broad shoulders, then down his smooth back, reveling in the feel of his supple skin and the way his taut muscles jumped beneath her fingertips.

He broke off their frantic kiss and dragged his open mouth down her throat. "So good," he muttered against her neck as his hands roamed her back. "You feel so damn good." He touched his tongue to the sensitive skin behind her ear and groaned. "Taste so damn good."

She would have returned the compliment, but his hands came forward to cup her breasts, evaporating her ability to speak. While his thumbs drew drugging circles around her nipples, he kissed his way along her collarbone and down her chest. Slipping his fingers beneath the straps of her chemise, he pulled the garment down to her waist where the bunched material floated in the gurgling water. She arched her back in a silent plea and gasped when he drew one aroused peak into the heat of his mouth. Her eyes slid closed, her head dropped back, and she fisted her fingers in his hair, urging him to take more of her, drowning in the pleasure of being touched, of touching. Of his mouth and hands on her, of her hands on him.

"Beautiful," he murmured against her breast, his voice a husky rasp in the darkness. He laved one nipple with a lazy swirl of his tongue while his fingers teased the other. His hand slipped beneath the water, lifted the hem of her chemise, and cupped her bare bottom. "So damn beautiful."

With his tongue lightly playing with hers and one hand caressing her breasts, his other hand slowly stroked her bottom, his fingers teasing the sensitive nerve endings between her cheeks. Unable to remain still, Genevieve lifted one leg and hooked it high on his hip, a blatant invitation he immediately took advantage of. The first touch of his fingers against her swollen folds dragged a guttural groan from her throat that felt as if it was ripped from her soul. Her head fell limply back and exhaling a long *aaaahhhh* of delight, she basked in the waves of pleasure washing through her. He slipped first one, then two fingers inside her and slowly pumped, eliciting another moan from her. Desperation seized her and she raised her leg higher, shifting so that his erection nestled directly against her throbbing clitoris. The pressure coiled the knot building inside her tighter and she writhed against him. He answered with a long, slow thrust of his hips that robbed her of the last vestiges of her control. Lifting her head, she fisted her hands in his hair. "More," she demanded against his mouth in a strained voice she barely recognized. "Please, more. *Now*."

He slipped a third finger inside her, deliciously stretching her. With his tongue stroking inside her mouth in unison to his thrusting fingers, her climax thundered through her. With a cry, she ground herself against him, saturated in sensation, adrift in pleasure. When the spasms tapered off to mere ripples, she melted like warmed wax, her rapid, shallow breaths pelting the side of his neck.

Still dazed, she felt his fingers slip from her body and her boneless leg slid from his hip. If not for his strong arm wrapped around her waist she would have slithered beneath the water.

He gently brushed his fingertips across her overheated cheek. "I wish it wasn't so bloody dark. I want to see you."

His words snapped her from the sated, languorous stupor into which she'd fallen, reminding her that it was only because of the darkness that this interlude had occurred. Only because of the darkness that she'd allowed herself to…

She squeezed her eyes shut. Dear God, she'd simply come apart in his arms, no inhibitions, no hesitation and utterly no control—indisputable proof of how desperately she missed being touched. If her ten years as Richard's mistress had taught her anything, it was how to seduce. Yet she'd been seduced by a single sentence. *Tell me it's not just me who feels this.* With one caress. By a man she barely knew. A man she'd selfishly taken pleasure from while offering him none—something she'd never done before. Something a mistress would never do.

You're not a mistress anymore, her inner voice whispered.

No. And she never would be, even if her hands were perfect. No man would ever own her again.

Still, guilt—along with a healthy dose of embarrassment—slapped her for so wantonly grabbing everything he offered, even demanding more, and giving nothing in return. She pulled in a fortifying breath, then lifted her head. In spite of the shadows, there was enough moonlight that she could see his eyes glittering. They appeared to devour her.

"I...I'm sorry, Mr. Cooper. I—"

He touched his fingers against her lips, cutting off her words. "Simon. Surely we're on a first-name basis now." There was no missing the hint of amusement in his voice. "Genevieve."

A tingle ran through her at the intimate timbre in his voice. "Very well, Simon. I'm sorry I was so... carried away."

"Are you?" He studied her and for a brief instant she wished for a flash of light so she could better see his expression. "You shouldn't be. I'm certainly not. You were...are...exquisite. Enchanting. Incredible." He leaned in and lightly scraped his teeth over her earlobe. "And absolutely delicious."

With her arms still loosely looped around his neck, Genevieve sighed with pleasure and tilted her head to afford him easier access to that neglected bit of skin she'd forgotten was so sensitive. "I'm not sorry for what happened between us—"

"I'm delighted to hear it. The pleasure was all mine."

"But that's just my point. And why I'm sorry. The pleasure was all *mine.*"

His warm lips traveled across her jaw. "I assure you it wasn't. The pleasure was mutual."

Genevieve leaned back in the circle of his arms. "It was?" Had she been so lost in her own release that she'd missed his?

He rolled his hips against her and she realized that the bulge pressing against her stomach, while still impressive, had indeed softened. "It was. I've been alone for…a while, and well, you are, as I said, exquisite. Hearing, seeing, feeling you climax was an impossible combination to resist."

There was no denying the feminine satisfaction that rippled through her. "So you decided to join me."

He huffed out a laugh. "I'm afraid there was nothing I could do to stop it. You are…" His hand came forward to cup her face. "Potent." Then his teeth flashed white in the darkness. "And besides, my breeches were already wet."

His smile faded and his expression turned serious. "As much as I wanted to be inside you, it's perhaps better that I wasn't. Contrary to my actions this evening, I am a cautious man. I don't normally allow my passions to rule me, and my mastery over myself is usually much more…"

"Masterful?" she suggested when he seemed at a loss. "Yes."

"Then I can only say I am glad you weren't left unsatisfied and flattered to have undone you so."

His gaze searched hers and he frowned. "Undone me. Yes, that's exactly what you did. And without any effort. Rather frightening to think what might happen if you actually put your wealth of feminine wiles into the effort."

"*Frightening* isn't the word I would use. I think *fascinating* would be a far better description." Feeling deliciously wicked, she rubbed her breasts against his chest, inwardly smiling at his swift intake of air.

"Indeed," he murmured, running his hands slowly up and down her bare back. "Especially now that the edge is off my ardor. I'll last longer next time."

"Next time? That sounds—"

"Presumptuous?" Before she could tell him that she was going to say *lovely,* he continued, "Yes, I know." He settled her more firmly against him. *Oh, my.* It seemed as if next time could happen very soon indeed. "But I've wanted you since the first moment I laid eyes on you. Make no mistake, Genevieve. I want to make love to you. But I have nothing to offer you beyond the fortnight I'll be in Little Longstone, which is something you must consider."

His gaze searched hers for several seconds. "Tonight we were both caught up in the moment. As much as I enjoy spontaneity, I don't act without considering the consequences of my actions. With any affair there can be repercussions. Even with discretion there can be scandal. I'll be gone, but you'll remain here and could face censure. And there's always the possibility of pregnancy. As much as I want you, I don't want you to make a decision in the heat of the moment that you'll regret. Think about it. There can be no doubt as to what I want, but it has to be right for you as well."

Genevieve stilled at the realization he was offering her not only himself, but a choice as well—a choice he wanted her to make with a clear mind. He was concerned enough to consider her position in Little Longstone as well as the possibility of pregnancy. And he was honest enough to let her know that should they enter into a liaison, it would only be of a temporary nature. She was very well aware that many men would neither have been so considerate nor given the situation any thought. They would have simply taken what was offered and damn the consequences, which for him would be minimal, but for her could be very costly.

There was no doubt he wanted her—the irrefutable proof was nestled against her belly. Yet he hadn't taken her, and God knows he could have—irrefutable proof he was a decent, honorable man. She'd only been with one other man in her life, and although she'd come to love Richard, she'd become his mistress out of necessity. And desperation. Because she hadn't had a choice, at least not one she was willing to contemplate. Now she had a choice, one she could make without her judgment being clouded by clawing, aching need.

There was a great deal to consider. She'd been able to hide her hands during this brief interlude, but the chances of her being able to do so over a fortnight were slim. Of course, as soon as he saw them, he'd no doubt reject her, which was a pain she didn't think she could bear. Not again.

"I appreciate your thoughtfulness, Simon. And your forbearance. I shall think on the matter." Indeed, she doubted she'd be able to think of anything else. "But now it's time for me to return home." She released him, slipped her hands under the water, then stepped back. His hands fell away from her and she immediately missed the feel of them on her skin. Turning her back to him, she lowered herself in the water up to her neck and quickly slipped her arms back into her chemise. After adjusting the garment, she moved onto the stone seat then stepped from the spring.

Her warm flesh instantly pebbled in the cool air and she reached for her robe, one corner of her mouth lifting at the sight of Beauty curled up next to her clothing. After knotting the sash around her waist, she donned her long cape, her gloves and her boots, and tucked her pistol into her pocket. Feeling far less vulnerable now that her hands were covered, she turned to face him. He'd emerged from the spring as well, and was tugging his jacket into place, watching her through hooded eyes. For several seconds they simply looked at each other and Genevieve experienced a pull of attraction, and something else…something she'd never before experienced. Something that made her want to run to him and bury her face against his broad chest. Breathe him in. Feel his strength. She wanted to hold him, and be held by him. And never let go. She frowned and shook her head to dispel it of the ridiculous notion.

"Are you cold?" he asked, walking toward her.

If only she were. She *should* be. Instead, heat rippled through her, increasing with every step closer he took. "No."

He stopped, looking at her as if she were a puzzle he couldn't solve. Then his gaze flicked to her mouth. Fire kindled in his eyes, and her heart lurched in anticipation. But instead of kissing her, he bent down and scooped up Beauty. The puppy opened one sleepy eye, gave a huge yawn, then snuggled into the curve of Simon's arm to dream doggie dreams.

Lightly petting the dog's golden head, Simon said softly, "Earlier, while dashing through the woods after this imp I was tempted to change her name to Evil Lead Chewer. Or Runs Impossibly Fast. Or Pain in the Arse. Now I'm tempted to change her name to Genius. Certainly I owe her the largest beef bone in the kingdom for leading me here."

"And here you thought she'd be nothing but trouble."

"Oh, she's trouble. But it appears I harbor a weakness for trouble." His gaze skimmed over her. "Among other things. Which means we should leave now. Lest we end up here all night." He extended his free arm. "Shall we?"

Genevieve tucked her hand in the crook of his elbow and they made their way along the path. For several minutes the only sound was that of their footfalls crunching against the fallen leaves. Then for reasons she didn't quite understand, she found herself admitting, "It's been a long time since I've walked through the woods with a man."

He turned his head to look at her. "I can only conclude that it's been your choice to walk alone because you'd have only to snap your fingers to find a dozen suitors knocking on your door."

Even though he was completely mistaken, warmth flooded Genevieve at the compliment. "Thank you, but you are far overestimating my charms, Simon."

"I'm not. *You* are far *under*estimating them. Have you no mirrors in your home?"

"Yes. And they don't lie." They showed her exactly what she was—an aging former mistress with ruined hands. A shell of the woman she once was.

"Then you must require spectacles."

She was about to assure him she didn't when he abruptly halted. They'd rounded a corner and her cottage was just ahead.

"Your front door is open," he said in an undertone, pulling her off the path and behind the trunk of an elm. As Genevieve peered through the darkness, he reached down and pulled a knife from his boot. The silver blade glinted in the moonlight. "Give me your pistol."

A chill ran through her at his terse whisper and she reached into her pocket. "That won't be necessary. It's not just a decoration—I'm very proficient."

"You're prepared to shoot someone?"

"If necessary."

He gave her a quick, appraising glance, then nodded. "Good. Let's hope you don't need to. Stay behind me, be prepared to run, and for God's sake don't shoot *me*."

He set the sleeping dog beneath the tree then crouching low, moved cautiously forward, his gaze scanning. Genevieve kept behind him, heart pounding with a combination of fear and dread. Was it possible Richard had come for the puzzle box? If so, she certainly didn't want Simon to hurt him, thinking him to be an intruder.

They reached the flagstone steps and approached the door, then stepped into the foyer. And were greeted by the sight of Baxter lying on the parquet floor, a dark trail of what could only be blood marring the side of his face.

10

WITH HIS GAZE scanning their surroundings, Simon knelt beside Baxter. Just as he touched his fingers to the side of the giant man's neck and felt his steady pulse, Baxter stirred and moaned.

"He's coming around," Simon said in a terse undertone. "I need to see if anyone's still in the house." Taking Genevieve by the shoulders, he backed her up several paces until her spine touched the paneling. "Stay here against the wall with your pistol at the ready until I return."

"But Baxter—"

"Will be fine until I return."

"I can't leave him like that on the floor."

"You won't be of any use to anyone if the intruder catches you unaware because you're tending to him. I won't be long."

After a brief hesitation, she nodded. With his knife at the ready, Simon quickly made his way through the house. His instincts told him the intruder was gone, and his search ascertained that was the case. The last room he checked before returning to the foyer was Genevieve's bedchamber. On a hunch he opened her dresser drawer and felt beneath the stacks of undergarments. His jaw clenched. He didn't know what else might have been taken from the house, but one thing was missing—the puzzle box was no longer hidden beneath her lingerie.

Had she moved it herself—or had the intruder taken it? He didn't believe for an instant that this was some random break-in. Someone else wanted that letter. But who? He didn't know, but he sure as hell was going to find out.

With his mouth flattened into a grim line, he hurried back to the foyer.

"The house is empty," Simon reported.

Genevieve immediately went to Baxter and dropped to her knees beside him. "He's groaned several times and just opened his eyes."

"Good. See to him and I'll be right back." Simon hurried outside and retrieved Beauty who mercifully still slept as she was carried into the foyer and set on a rug in the corner. Simon then knelt beside Genevieve who was gently dabbing the wound on Baxter's head with a lacy handkerchief. "How is he?"

"Conscious." No sooner had she uttered the word than Baxter attempted to sit up. Simon immediately urged him back down.

"Bloody hell, me head feels like a battalion of demons are stabbing me skull with their pitchforks," Baxter said in a gravelly voice. He groaned and slammed his eyes shut. "What the hell sort of rotgut did I drink?"

"You didn't drink anything," Genevieve said. "You were knocked unconscious."

Baxter opened one eye and frowned. "Unconscious?"

"By someone who made a thorough and not very neat search of the house," Simon said grimly as he leaned closer to examine the egg-sized lump on the side of Baxter's bald head. He turned to Genevieve. "We need some light."

She rose and returned less than a minute later bearing an oil lamp that cast the foyer in a golden glow. After looking at Baxter's wound, Simon said, "It's stopped bleeding. But that's a hell of a lump you've got there."

Baxter grunted. "Hell of a headache I've got."

"Did you see who hit you?"

Baxter tried to shake his head, winced, then said, "No. I were tossin' and turnin' and heard a crashing sound, like glass breakin'. Thought it might be Sophia getting into some mischief, so I came to check." His gaze shifted to Genevieve. "Didn't want to think of you cuttin' yer feet in the mornin'. Next thing I know, I'm starin' up at you with me head feelin' two yards thick." His eyes widened. "Bastard wot hit me didn't hurt you, Gen, did he?"

She shook her head. "No. I'm fine."

Baxter's gaze turned to Simon and his eyes narrowed to slits. "Just wot the bloody hell are *you* doin' here?"

"I was escorting Genevieve home. When we arrived, the door was open and we found you lying here."

"Escortin' her home?" Baxter once again struggled to sit up, this time accomplishing the task with Simon and Genevieve's assistance. After taking several slow breaths, he turned to Simon with a baleful expression. "She already *was* home. So maybe *yer* the one who nearly broke me skull."

Before Simon could reply, Genevieve said quietly, "I'd left the house. To go to the springs. Simon was walking Beauty and they happened upon me."

Baxter blinked. "Wot in God's name were ye thinkin' to be going off to the springs at night by yerself?"

"I took my pistol and was prepared to shoot any lurkers."

"Ye didn't shoot *him*," Baxter grumbled, glowering at Simon.

"I wasn't lurking," Simon said lightly. "But someone was." He recalled the sensation of being watched he'd experienced at the festival. Turning to Genevieve, he asked, "Have there been any robberies in the area lately?"

"Not that I'm aware of."

"You need to go through the house, see if anything was stolen. Do you have any valuables?"

Something flickered in her eyes. "A few pieces of jewelry, but nothing worth a great deal."

"Let's get Baxter cleaned and bandaged, then we'll check to see if anything is missing."

While Genevieve went to gather the bandages, Simon assisted Baxter to his feet, nearly staggering under the man's considerable weight as he helped him to the sitting room.

"Don't think I don't know wot yer up to," Baxter muttered as they made their way slowly down the corridor.

"Up to?"

"I seen the way ye look at her."

"And how is that?"

"Like she's a pork chop and yer a starvin' mongrel." Baxter halted and jerked his arm from Simon's grasp. He swayed on his feet and slapped a beefy hand against the wall to steady himself. Shooting Simon a dark scowl surely meant to reduce him to dust, he said, "I won't let ye hurt her."

"I've no intention of hurting her." Indeed, Simon hoped his investigations would prove that Genevieve's reasons for removing the letter from the alabaster box were harmless and that she was innocent of any wrongdoings.

"Don't matter wot yer intentions are, ye could do it

just the same, and she don't deserve it. She's been hurt enough." Baxter leaned forward. "If you hurt *her*, I'm going to hurt *you*. Consider yerself warned."

Simon didn't doubt for a moment that Baxter could crush his skull like a walnut with his bare hands. Luckily, thanks to his training and experience as a spy, he excelled at extricating himself from dangerous situations. He'd been threatened by bigger men than Baxter.

"Fine. I'm warned. Now let's see to getting that head wound cleaned so you're better able to protect her— from whoever broke into the house."

Baxter made a sound that resembled a growl and resumed walking slowly. "The bastard will be damn sorry when I get my hands on him. Wot I want to know is wot the hell was she thinkin', wanderin' around the woods at night? And why the bloody hell were you walkin' yer dog on her property? Spyin' on her, were ye?"

"No, I was chasing my ill-mannered puppy whose razor-sharp teeth bit through her lead. I'm lucky I didn't have to chase the beast to Scotland. Be glad, at least for tonight, that Genevieve wasn't here. She might have ended up unconscious like you. Or worse." A shudder ran through him at the thought.

They entered the sitting room and Baxter plopped down heavily on the settee in front of the fireplace. Genevieve entered seconds later carrying a bowl of water and several lengths of clean linen. Moving directly toward Baxter, she said to Simon, "I'll take care of him. There's a bottle of whiskey in the bottom drawer of the desk. Could you please pour some for Baxter? And help yourself if you'd like."

Simon crossed to the desk. There were two bottom drawers, one on each side of the chair. Thanks to his earlier searches of the house he knew which one contained the bottle of whiskey. While he poured a generous portion for Baxter and a fingerful for himself, he watched Genevieve gently cleanse away the blood with a steady hand. A steady *gloved* hand. Clearly not even Baxter saw her without her gloves, and once again, he wondered what sort of injury she was hiding. He recalled the feel of her fingers sifting through his hair at the spring, her hands caressing him, and heat suffused him. Whatever it was, it didn't lessen the fact that her touch set him on fire.

Carrying the two drinks, he walked to the settee and handed Baxter his glass. The giant grunted his thanks then proceeded to gulp down the potent liquor in two quick swallows. "Am I goin' to need stitchin' up, Gen?"

Genevieve lifted the oil lamp to examine the wound then shook her head. "Not this time." She offered him a soft smile. "That's nice for a change."

Curiosity pinched Simon, urging him to ask how Genevieve and Baxter had come to be together, the refined woman and the ruffian, but he shoved aside the urge—for now. Better to wait until he and Genevieve were alone. Instead he asked, "Baxter gets struck on the head regularly?"

"No," Genevieve said, wiping away the blood that had dripped down Baxter's face with a calm expertise that indicated it wasn't the first time she'd performed such ministrations. "At least not recently. But he had his share of altercations in his youth that resulted in some injuries."

Baxter guffawed. "Other blokes always ended up lookin' worse than me, though, didn't they, Gen?"

Her lips twitched. "Always."

Baxter's rough features collapsed into a frown.

"'Cept this time. That's going to be one sorry bugger when I get ahold of him. Good thing I weren't sleeping. It were better I heard the bastard and scared him off—even if me head had to pay the price."

He winced when Genevieve applied some ointment to his wound and she immediately asked, clearly to distract him from the discomfort, "Why couldn't you sleep? Are you unwell?"

To Simon's amazement the giant appeared to blush. "Um, ah, me mind was, er, occupied."

A knowing glint entered Genevieve's eyes. "I think I can guess with what, or rather, with whom. Miss Winslow is a lovely young woman."

Baxter's blush extended to the top of his bald head. "Far too good for the likes of me."

"I disagree, and you'd best be careful what you say about my dear friend, Baxter," Genevieve said, winding a long strip of linen around his head, "or else I'll be forced to give you another whack to knock some sense into you." She tucked in the end of the strip then leaned back to examine her handiwork. "How do you feel?"

"Like a bloody idiot for bein' caught unawares."

She smiled. "I meant your head."

"Poundin' like the hammers of hell, but I've had worse headaches after a night swillin' Blue Ruin."

"Glad you're all right," Simon broke in, in spite of his interest in the byplay between the two, which made it clear they were more friends than employer and servant. He couldn't imagine any of his staff ever speaking to him in the casual manner that Baxter addressed Genevieve. He tried to envision Ramsey or his valet or his man of affairs calling him Simon and utterly failed. "Now let's see if anything was stolen."

While Baxter remained in the sitting room nursing another glass of whiskey, Simon followed Genevieve through the house, helping her straighten up things the intruder had disturbed. She found nothing missing, not even her few pieces of jewelry which she kept in a locked box in her small sitting room—a box which had been forced open.

When they entered Genevieve's bedchamber, Sophia lifted her head from the spot where she lay curled up on the counterpane. After offering a half-hearted yawn, she settled back down.

Standing in the doorway, Simon's gaze drifted to the statue in the corner and a vivid image flashed through his mind of hiding behind the marble woman and watching Genevieve—a real woman who, in spite of all the reasons why she shouldn't, had captured his imagination and ignited his fantasies.

He pulled his attention back to Genevieve, who was hurrying across the room to her dresser. Simon followed, watching as she yanked open the drawer where the puzzle box had been. She pawed through her lingerie which the intruder—and Simon—had already disturbed, then drew in a shuddering breath. She whispered something that sounded like *bastard*, but he couldn't be certain.

"Something missing?" he asked.

She hesitated then said, "I…I'm just distressed that someone has been touching my things." She looked through the remainder of the drawers, then slowly turned to face him. Her skin was pale and although she was clearly unsettled, she was also obviously angry.

"Well?" he asked, looking into her eyes, hoping she wouldn't lie to him, but knowing she would.

Her gaze never wavered. "Nothing is missing."

Disappointment rippled through him. She had no reason to trust him—indeed, she was wise not to, even though she didn't know that. Still, he'd hoped she would confide in him. Pushing the unreasonable feeling away, he said, "If this was merely a robbery, the intruder would have taken your jewelry. He was looking for something specific. Do you have any idea what?"

Again she hesitated, and for a single heartbeat, he thought she might perhaps tell him. Then she shook her head. "No." Then something that looked like satisfaction flickered in her eyes. "But whatever it was, he didn't find it."

"How do you know?"

She blinked, clearly nonplussed. Then she shrugged. "Because there was nothing to find."

Hope flared in him. He didn't doubt that she was telling the truth with that statement. The letter was still here. The intruder hadn't found it because she'd removed it from the box. Which meant not only that Simon still had the chance to retrieve the letter, but also that the bastard who'd broken in tonight would most likely be back.

All the protective instincts that she'd aroused in him from his first look at her roared to life. She needed protection. And he would make certain she received it. At least until he had his letter.

You want a hell of a lot more from her than that letter and you damn well know it, his conscience whispered. Bloody annoying voice. He needed to teach it how to lie. Shouldn't be difficult considering what an accomplished liar Simon was—a skill his years as a spy had honed to a razor-sharp edge. Yet, for reasons he refused to examine lying wasn't sitting well with him at the moment. Which was ridiculous, especially since she'd lied to him.

Consigning his irritating thoughts to the devil, he said, "We can report the break-in to the magistrate tomorrow. In the meantime, you can't stay here."

She raised her brows. "Surely you don't think whoever did this will be back?" Even as she said the words, he could see the realization dawning on her that it was, indeed, a very real possibility.

"I don't think it can be ruled out. Which means that you—and Baxter and Sophia as well—are coming home with me."

For several seconds she said nothing, just looked at him with an annoyingly inscrutable expression. Damn it, why couldn't she be like the other women he knew—predictable and easy to read? She moistened her lips, a gesture that drew his gaze to her gorgeous mouth—a mouth he ached to taste again.

"That is very kind, but—"

He jerked his gaze back up to hers. "No buts. There is ample room for all of you in my cottage, and you'll be safe there." He would see to it. Because the thought of anything happening to her, of her being hurt the way Baxter had been, twisted his insides into knots. "Baxter isn't fully recovered, and even if he were, based on the amount of whiskey he's tossed back, he's in no condition to properly protect you. He requires rest. And you…" Reaching out, he lightly grasped her shoulders. "You require someone to watch over you."

She stilled beneath his hands. For an instant he believed she was going to pull away and he had to fight the urge to tighten his hold. But instead she raised her chin. "While I'm perfectly capable of, and accustomed to, taking care of myself, I cannot deny I am unnerved by what's happened. Therefore I accept your offer, with my thanks." She lifted a single brow. "I must say, for a steward, you've proven unusually capable in dealing with this matter." Her gaze flicked to his boot. "And you're surprisingly at ease handling that knife."

He shrugged. "When you work for a wealthy man, you become adept at dispatching hooligans and foot-pads and the like."

"I see. Well, if you'll excuse me, I'll change my clothes so we can depart. Would you mind sitting with Baxter while I do? I hate to think of him all alone."

Simon nodded then released her. And was alarmed at how difficult it was to do so. He turned to go, but instead of leaving, he nodded toward the statue. "That's a beauti-ful piece." *That I stood behind and fantasized about you.*

"Thank you. It was a gift."

"From your husband?"

"No. From myself. I saw her in a London shop years ago and had to have her. The beauty and simplicity in her lines, in her pose, captivated me. I couldn't resist her."

Simon pulled his gaze from the statue to look at her. *I couldn't resist her.* "Yes. I understand completely. Baxter and I will await you in the sitting room." With that, he turned and quickly quit the room, before he gave in to the temptation to yank her into his arms and put out the simmering fire that seemed to crackle beneath his skin.

He strode down the corridor and dragged his hands down his face. Bloody hell! As if the searing attraction he felt toward her wasn't bad enough, this fierce pro-tectiveness was utter insanity. And it could very well prove dangerous. She'd lied to him, most recently about the puzzle box. She knew the box had been stolen and she knew where the letter she'd removed from it was. His every instinct should be warning him away from her; instead a small voice in his head insisted there was some reasonable explanation. And that she wasn't in any way involved in Ridgemoor's death.

Damn it, and now she'd be staying in his temporary home. Close enough to touch. And, by God, he wanted to touch her, *wanted* her, with a raw ferocity he couldn't recall ever before experiencing. Their interlude at the hot springs had only served to whet his appetite for her.

He'd offered her a choice. Only now did he realize that by doing so, he may have gained strides in earning her trust, a trust that could lead to her confiding to him the whereabouts of the letter. However, at the time he made the offer, he hadn't been thinking of his mission. Not at all. No, all he'd thought of was her. What was best for her. How best not to hurt her or involve her in any scandal.

It was the first time he'd ever forgotten his mission. Ever allowed a woman to distract him from his purpose. And the first time since he was a green lad he had so completely lost control of himself and his passions.

Which meant that regardless of whether Genevieve Ralston was guilty of any wrongdoing, she was very dangerous indeed.

_11_

GENEVIEVE paced her bedchamber in Simon's cottage. A low-burning fire in the hearth warmed the small but comfortable room, and the bed, with its forest-green counterpane and trio of pillows looked cozy and inviting. Baxter was settled in another bedchamber, asleep seconds after his head touched the pillow. Sophia, initially unhappy at the change of environment and completely disdainful of Beauty, now lay curled up in a drowsy ball on the hearthrug, allowing the fire's warmth to worship her. There wasn't a single reason for Genevieve not to slip beneath the covers and go to sleep.

No reason except the whirlwind of thoughts spinning through her mind in regard to tonight's break-in and its ramifications. And in regard to Simon Cooper.

She'd paced the length of the room for the past two hours, trying to make sense of tonight's events. Yet all her pacing had only resulted in a plethora of unanswered questions. She'd initially considered the break-in to be a further threat against Charles Brightmore, but she'd discarded that idea the instant she'd discovered the alabaster box missing. Richard's note had stated he would come for the box. Had he visited the cottage tonight—or had he sent someone in his place? But surely Richard wouldn't have hurt Baxter. Perhaps he hadn't realized it was him—although who else would her former lover have thought would be in her house? Then again, she hadn't believed Richard capable of hurting *her* the way he had, and she'd been proven profoundly wrong about that.

If the intruder was someone acting on Richard's behalf, that meant Richard hadn't wanted to see her. Had he suspected she'd intended to confront him, force him to utter the words he'd been too cowardly to say to her face? Or had Richard himself come to her bedchamber under the cover of darkness to regain the puzzle box and the letter hidden inside? Her instincts told her no. Richard had proven himself too weak to do something as violent as strike someone—especially a man who outweighed him by at least five stone. And he'd made it perfectly clear he no longer desired her. Therefore why risk encountering her in her bedchamber? Unless he'd been spying on her and knew she'd left the house.

The questions that had plagued her since she'd received the box once again drifted through her mind. Why had Richard sent it to her? What was the significance of the letter she'd found hidden inside? Richard was a powerful man, a growing force in politics. The letter was obviously very important to him, enough that he'd entrusted it to her for safekeeping. Why?

The more she thought on the matter, the more convinced she was that Richard himself wasn't the intruder. And that led to the question—was the culprit acting for Richard, or against him? Richard had written that she was the only one he could trust. Were the puzzle box and the letter hidden inside important to someone other than him? Were they important enough that a man would be attacked and her home ransacked? And would the intruder be back when he realized that although he'd stolen the box, he hadn't found the letter?

She experienced a small thrill of triumph over that, but then quickly sobered. Perhaps it would have been better if the letter *had* been found. Anger seethed through her that someone had hurt Baxter, had violated her home, her sanctuary and had pawed through her personal possessions. If the letter had been found, then she'd no longer be involved in whatever this madness was and she could simply concentrate on her own life.

Which brought her back to Simon Cooper.

Genevieve paused in her pacing to stare into the flames dancing in the hearth. Dear God, she was consumed with thoughts of him, her body on fire for wanting him. There were reasons why she shouldn't enter into a liaison with him, but every time her mind listed them, her heart discarded them.

He was a stranger. *Who'd proven himself charming, disarming, witty, generous, and brave. He was a hard-working man—not a bored aristocrat.* She had secrets she couldn't share. *He hasn't made any demands or asked you to share anything…except your body.* He'd be leaving Little Longstone in two weeks' time. *I'm not looking for a long-term arrangement, so why not enjoy him for the short time he's here?*

Why not, indeed?

In the *Ladies' Guide,* she had advised Today's Modern Woman that the best way to forget one man, to exorcise him from one's mind, was to have another man. Although truth be known, except for his connection to the puzzle box, she hadn't spared Richard a single thought since first laying eyes on Simon.

Simon…

She heaved the sort of gushy, feminine sigh she'd believed herself long past releasing. Their interlude in the springs had opened a door she'd firmly slammed when Richard had left her, one she'd not only planned never to open again, but one she'd never dreamed of having the opportunity to open. Of course, as Simon had pointed out, there was the possibility of scandal should anyone discover their affair. But she knew how to be discreet, and given his concern for the matter, she didn't doubt he did as well. As for pregnancy, she was well-acquainted with the various methods of preventing it. But given her courses were due to begin in only a few days, she wasn't concerned on that score.

No, her hesitation all boiled down to one thing. She glanced down at her gloves. At the hot spring, she'd been able to submerge her hands in the water, but here there was nowhere to hide. Thanks to her soak in the warm water and a liberal application of her cream, the ache in her joints right now was minimal. Yet by morning she knew the stiffness and swelling would return. Of course, she didn't have to spend the entire night in his bed...

It would only take a few hours, in the dark, to put out this fire he'd ignited inside her, an inferno that was consuming her. Rather than sating her, her earlier climax had only served to further fuel her hunger. So long as they remained in darkness, she could keep her hands hidden. And they could enjoy each other for the short time he was here. She never thought she'd have the opportunity to be with a man again, never believed that any man would desire her again. The fact that Simon did, and that she wanted him so badly...it was a temptation she simply couldn't resist.

Thus resolved, she quietly left her room and walked down the corridor, halting in front of the door leading to Simon's bedchamber. Was he asleep? Or was he, like her, restless and aroused and consumed with desire.

Only one way to find out, her inner voice urged her.

She debated knocking, but instead slowly turned the brass handle. The door silently opened and she slipped inside, closing the oak panel then turning the key in the lock. No fire burned in the grate and the curtains were drawn, cloaking the room in deep shadows. The room was cool from the lack of a fire and smelled of Simon—clean, with a hint of sandalwood.

She hesitated, waiting for her eyes to adjust to the darkness. And suddenly she saw him, or rather the shadowy outline of him, rising from a chair set before the empty hearth. With her heart pounding she watched him approach. It was so dark she couldn't make out his features until he halted directly in front of her. Then she saw the desire in his eyes, felt the heat pumping off him. That warmth, the delicious scent of him all but rendered her woozy with yearning.

"I was hoping you'd come," he said quietly. "You're certain?"

"I wouldn't be here if I wasn't. But I have two requests."

Simon pulled in a slow, unsteady breath. He'd sat in the dark for the last two hours, watching the fire burn to ashes, wanting her, his body aching for her, willing her to come to him, and more afraid than he cared to admit that she wouldn't. And now here she was. Bloody hell, it was all he could do not to simply jerk her into his arms and drag her to the floor.

"I'll do everything I can to grant them," he said.

Indeed, he couldn't imagine denying her anything. "Tell me what you want."

"Darkness."

He pushed aside his twinge of disappointment. He wanted, very much to see her every movement, each expression, her gorgeous eyes dilated with passion. "Very well, although I'm sorry not to be able to see you better." Forcing himself to move slowly, he reached out and untied the ribbon from the bottom of her braid then sifted his fingers through her hair. Soft curls spilled over his wrists, releasing the delicate scent of roses. He wrapped silky strands around his fist then brought them to his face to breathe deeply of their floral fragrance. "What is your second request?"

"Earlier tonight you pleasured me. If you'll recall from your reading of the *Ladies' Guide,* Today's Modern Woman should strive to return pleasure when pleasure is given. Therefore, I wish to return the favor and pleasure you."

She settled her hands on his abdomen and he sucked in a quick breath. Even through his linen shirt her touch set his skin ablaze.

"I don't believe you'll find that a difficult task."

"Perhaps not, but you'll allow me?"

"My darling Genevieve, you have my permission to take any liberties with my body that you so choose. Far be it for me to contradict the desires of Today's Modern Woman. Especially when they so precisely match my own."

"*Any* liberties?"

"Yes." God, yes.

"Excellent." Even the darkness couldn't completely hide the slow smile that curved her lips, speeding up his already pounding heart. She lightly grasped his wrists and settled his hands at his side. "All you need to do is remain still…and enjoy."

"Enjoying won't present any problem, but remaining still…" His words tapered off when she began slowly pulling his shirt from his breeches. "That is going to prove a challenge."

"I thought you harbored a weakness for challenges."

"I do, however, there are challenges, and then there are—" This time his words ended on a quick intake of breath as her hands slid beneath the linen to lightly stroke his torso.

"There are what?" she murmured, leaning forward to press her lips to his throat.

"There are…" His muscles jumped beneath her fingers. "Yes?"

He huffed out a laugh. "I've no idea. What was the question?"

Her fingers lightly circled the skin just above the waistband of his breeches. "You're very easily distracted, Simon."

"No, I'm not. At least, not usually." Actually, never. She slipped a single fingertip just beneath his waistband and trailed it across his pelvis. "The problem is that you're, ah, very distracting."

"How like a man to blame someone else."

"I'll accept blame where needed. However, it's hardly my fault that you're so incredibly…" He pulled in another quick breath when her fingers coasted over his nipples.

"So incredibly what?"

"Um…distracting. I think. What were we talking about?"

She laughed softly, and slipped her hands from beneath his shirt, which he didn't like, but it at least restored a bit of his ability to concentrate. "Raise your arms," she said.

"Clearly Today's Modern Woman likes to give orders."

"Yes, we do. Those who obey are rewarded handsomely."

"And those who don't?"

She gently bit his earlobe and he could have sworn his eyes glazed over. "Are dealt with very harshly."

"I'm certain that's supposed to be meant as some sort of threat, yet you manage to make *harshly* sound extremely enticing."

"Good. I want you enticed."

"Be assured that I am."

She brushed her pelvis against his erection. "Yes, I can see—and feel—that you are."

"Entirely your fault, I'm afraid. I've been in an almost constant state of arousal since the first time I saw you. It's become rather a problem."

"How interesting that where you see a problem, I see only…opportunity. Don't worry, Simon. I've every intention of taking care of that problem for you."

"I can't think of a single instance in my entire life when I've heard better news."

"Now raise your arms."

He obeyed and with a bit of help from him, she pulled his shirt over his head then glided her hands over his chest. "Put your hands behind your back."

Her sultry tone quickened his pulse and again he obeyed. She bent down then moved to stand behind him. He felt something soft and cool slip over his wrists. Realization hit him and he sucked in a quick breath. "You're *tying* me?"

"You did say *any* liberties, Simon. I thought since you'd mentioned that particular section in the *Ladies' Guide,* you'd be intrigued. Are you reneging?"

Her voice was a heated purr next to his ear that shot fiery vibrations to his every cell. He recalled the fantasy she'd inspired the first time he'd seen her, wet and nearly naked in her bedchamber, his imaginings fueled by the words in the *Ladies' Guide.*

"Not reneging," he assured her.

"Good." She finished with the ribbon and he gave his hands an experimental tug. Snug, but not tight. Certainly escapable for a man of his experience. Yet he had absolutely no desire to free himself.

She moved to stand in front of him. "For someone who spends most of his time sitting behind a desk poring over ledgers, you are very nicely made," she murmured.

He opened his mouth to reply, but his words turned into a groan when she pressed her lips to the center of his chest then dragged her open mouth to his nipple. "To what do you attribute your excellent fitness?" she asked, interspersing each word with nipping kisses to his chest, all while her hands gently stroked his skin.

"Horses," he managed to say. "Ride horses."

Her tongue drew a lazy circle around his nipple. "So you like to ride."

"Yes. Actually, I used to think it was one of my favorite things—until I felt your, *ahhhh,* tongue on me."

"You like my tongue on you?"

"*Like* is an extremely lukewarm word to describe it."

"Good. Because I liked your tongue on me."

"Excellent. In case you harbored any doubts, my tongue can't wait to be on you again."

"That's good to know. And quite obvious." One hand came forward to stroke the length of his erection.

Simon sucked in a harsh breath, one that locked in his throat when he felt her opening his breeches. Her hands slipped beneath the buckskin and his smalls, slowly dragging both over his hips then down his legs, and he was eternally grateful he'd removed his boots and stockings earlier so few obstacles impeded her disrobing him. He stepped out of the garments and nudged them aside with his bare foot. Then he waited, utterly still, naked except for the satin ribbon binding his hands, and harder than he'd ever been in his entire life. His every muscle tensed in an agony of anticipation.

"Oh, my," she murmured. "This is indeed a problem. An *enormous* problem."

Bloody hell, she had no idea. And if she didn't touch him soon, he was going to—

The first stroke of her fingers over his erection erased every thought from his mind and he released his pent-up breath on a long hiss of pleasure. She wrapped her fingers around him and gently squeezed and he gritted his teeth against the overwhelming urge to thrust into her hand. "You cannot imagine how good that feels."

"On the contrary, thanks to the way you touched me at the spring, I know precisely how good it feels."

She stroked him slowly, her fingers relentless, caressing his length then circling the head. He strained against his bindings, and unable to help himself, he rolled his hips, pressing himself into her palm.

She leaned forward and nipped at his bottom lip. "You're supposed to remain still."

He wanted to assure her he was trying, but she robbed him of his ability to speak when she eased one hand between his legs to cup him. With a growl of approval he widened his stance and dropped his head back. And tried his damnedest not to move.

Bloody hell, her hands were pure magic, conjuring sensations that threatened to bring him to his knees. Just when he thought he couldn't take another stroke, she released him and trailed her fingers over his abdomen.

He dragged in a shuddering breath and fought for control. "I'm a heartbeat away from unraveling."

Her finger slowly circled his navel. "Somehow that doesn't sound like a complaint."

"It's not. It's a promise—for retribution."

"You mean like an eye for an eye?"

"No. I mean a stroke for a stroke. A caress for a caress. A kiss for a kiss. A lick for a lick."

"So you intend to give as good as you get?"

"The instant you untie me and release me from my promise to remain still."

She wrapped her fingers around him again and lightly stroked. "You're doing extremely well at remaining immobile."

"*Ahhhhh*...the effort is costing me, believe me. I'm not certain how much more I can take."

"Let's find out." With that, she leaned in and slowly kissed her way down his torso. Her warm breath tickled his skin, igniting fires, while her fingers lightly caressed his spine. She moved lower, her lips and tongue drifting over him, exploring his navel, then lower, touching him everywhere except where he most wanted. By the time she dropped to her knees, his breathing had turned into a series of ragged pants and his fingers were numb from clenching them so tightly.

He felt her touch a single fingertip to the head of his

jutting cock. "You're wet," she whispered, spreading the moisture with a lazy circular motion.

He cleared his throat to locate his voice. "It's only by sheer will that I'm not wetter—"

His words were chopped off when she leaned forward and treated the length of his erection to a long, slow lick. Simon's jaw clenched and he fought for control as she grasped his shaft and teased the sensitive head with swirling strokes of her tongue.

"You're driving me...*ahhhh*...mad," he managed to utter in a hoarse voice.

"Mad in a good way, I hope."

"Again, *good* is a very lukewarm description."

"Then let's try for *incredible,*" she whispered and drew him deep into her mouth.

Tight wet heat surrounded him, ripping a growl from his throat. Inwardly cursing the darkness that obscured his view, he closed his eyes and imagined the sight of her plump lips surrounding him, moving over him. White-hot pleasure sliced through him, every sensation somehow rendered even more intense by the fact that he couldn't touch her in return. Her tongue circled him, shooting fire through him, gathering heat in the base of his spine. The combination of her swirling tongue, her mouth milking him, and her fingers fondling and stroking between his legs and over his buttocks quickly propelled him to the edge and all too soon he teetered on the brink of release.

Her lips tightened around him, drawing on him so tightly he swore he was going to implode.

"No more," he said, his voice sounding as if he'd swallowed gravel. "Can't take anymore." With a hard jerk and twist of his wrists he broke free of his satin restraints. Grasping her shoulders he gently pushed her back until she released him. He was a single touch away from coming, and he wanted to be inside her, feel her body clamped around him when he climaxed.

He urged her to her feet, lifted her night rail over her head and tossed the garment aside. Again cursing the darkness that hid her from him, he skimmed his hands over her warm, soft flesh and discovered she wore nothing else save skin. His hands, normally so steady, felt decidedly shaky, certainly too much so to contend with tiny buttons and layers of clothing. Bending his knees, he scooped her up and strode to the bed.

"I wasn't quite finished pleasuring you," she murmured, lightly biting his neck.

"If I were any more pleasured, *I'd* be finished. So now it's your turn. Turnabout is only fair." He set her on the edge of the bed then knelt on the floor, his shoulders splaying her thighs wide. Her scent, an intoxicating combination of roses and female musk hit him like a shot of straight brandy to an empty stomach. He ran one hand up her body, easing her onto her back then reached out to trail a single fingertip along the seam of her sex, eliciting a groan from both of them. Bloody hell, she was drenched. "Seems I'm not the only one who's wet," he said, teasing her with a light, circular motion.

"Since the moment I first saw you," she whispered. "And as a Modern Woman I insist you do something about it. Immediately."

He slipped two fingers inside her tight heat. "You, my dear, are extremely demanding."

She writhed against his hand and groaned. "Yes, I am. Do you truly wish to complain about that?"

"Absolutely not. As far as I'm concerned, naked, wet

and demanding is the perfect combination of traits. Long live Today's Modern Woman. And retribution."

He eased his fingers from her and a dark smile curved his lips at her mewl of protest, a sound that turned into a gasp when he slid his hands beneath her bottom, set her thighs over his shoulders and lifted her to his mouth.

His lips, tongue and fingers teased her folds, swirling, tasting, nibbling, licking, delving while he absorbed her moans, relentlessly coaxing her toward release, determined to give her as much pleasure as she'd given him. When she climaxed, she arched her back and cried out his name in a hoarse voice that echoed through him.

The instant her spasms tapered off, he rose and lifted her, settling her head on his pillow. Unable to wait another instant, he covered her body with his and entered her with one smooth thrust. Her slick walls held him like a velvet fist and for several seconds he remained still, his eyes shut, absorbing the incredible feel of her.

"Tight," he murmured against her mouth. He withdrew nearly all the way out of her body then slowly sank deep again. "Wet. Soft. Hot." Withdrawal and another slow, deep plunge. "You feel so damn *good.*"

She released a long, guttural moan and wrapped her legs around his waist. "More," she whispered, clutching his shoulders. *"More."*

That impatient, husky demand incinerated whatever remnants of control Simon had managed to hold on to. He increased the tempo and force of his thrusts. Mindless, gritting his teeth against the white-hot pleasure, he sank into her again and again, lost in a dark, fiery abyss where nothing existed except her. The instant she arched beneath him he let himself go, thrusting deep, her silky sheath convulsing around him as shudders wracked him. When the spasms subsided, he buried his face in the fragrant curve where her neck and shoulder met and fought to catch his breath.

Bloody hell, how was it possible to feel so completely wrung out, yet so…reborn? Better than reborn. He felt…new. Like tarnished silver that had been polished after decades of neglect. He'd enjoyed his fair share of lovers in the past, experienced women who knew how to please a man and receive pleasure in return. But something about this woman left him satisfied in a way he'd never felt before.

When his breathing had calmed to something close to normal, he lifted his head. He immediately sensed how still she'd gone and he once again cursed the darkness that kept him from seeing her clearly. While he'd been taking his time catching his breath, he'd no doubt been squashing her. He made to roll off her, but she tightened her arms and legs around him.

"Don't go," she whispered. "The way you feel on top of me, inside of me…I'm not ready for it to end."

Heaven help him, neither was he. He brushed his fingers over her cheek, freezing when he felt the wetness on her soft skin. "Are you *crying?*" When she didn't answer, his fingertips explored further and his heart squeezed. "You *are* crying. Damn it, did I hurt you?"

She shook her head. "No." She trailed her fingers over his features, as if trying to memorize them in the dark. "I'm just…overwhelmed. I…never expected to feel that way again. Never expected to experience passion again." She turned her head and kissed his palm, a tender gesture that seemed to yank his heart from its moorings. "Thank you, Simon."

His throat tightened at the emotion in her voice. "Genevieve." Bloody hell, just saying her name pleased him. He leaned forward and touched his forehead to hers. "I am the one who should be thanking you."

For several seconds she said nothing. He listened to her pull in a several deep breaths, her warm exhalations caressing his lips. Then he felt her lips curve against his palm. "I must say, your idea of retribution gives an entirely new meaning to the phrase *revenge is sweet.*"

"Indeed it is. And I'm delighted you think so, since I'm not nearly finished with my retribution."

"Oh, my. But surely you realize that will only lead to me enacting retribution of my own."

"Yes, that did occur to me." He heaved a dramatic sigh and nuzzled her fragrant neck. "I'll endeavor to endure whatever repayment you deem appropriate."

"As I recall, your method involves a kiss for a kiss."

"Yes. And a touch for a touch—"

"And a lick for a lick?"

"Precisely. And then there is the small matter of the satin ribbons to bind the wrists."

She heaved a dramatic sigh. "And if I refuse to give in to such treacherous demands?"

"I'll simply have to find a way to bring you around to my point of view."

"Hmm…I suspect that won't be overly difficult. I have a terrible weakness for kisses."

He ran his tongue over her plump bottom lip. "And licking?"

"A *very* terrible weakness."

"As I said, I'll try not to complain and take it like a man." Yet as he settled his mouth over hers, Simon was hit by the unsettling realization that he had a very terrible weakness of his own. And she was named Genevieve Ralston.

12

Simon awakened and moaned in protest at the evaporation of his very enjoyable, very erotic dream featuring him, Genevieve and a jar of honey. But then he realized it didn't actually have to end. She was right here in his bed. And there were several jars of honey in the pantry.

Smiling, he rolled over, then froze at the sight of the empty space next to him.

Muttering an obscenity, he flung off the covers and grabbed his breeches. Damn it, he was supposed to be protecting her. How the hell had she managed to leave the room without awakening him? He was normally a very light sleeper, but clearly not this morning. Was she safe?

He jabbed his legs into his breeches, snatched his knife from the bedside table then quickly crossed the room on silent bare feet. As soon as he stepped into the corridor, he heard the murmur of voices. Keeping close to the wall, he moved cautiously forward. As he approached the kitchen he heard Baxter say, "That ain't a smart thing to do."

"You're looking for trouble" came Genevieve's voice.

Clutching his knife tighter, Simon crept forward then cautiously peered around the corner. And blinked.

Genevieve sat at the wooden table in the center of the kitchen, a plate of food and steaming teacup in front of her. Baxter stood next to her, a white apron covering the front of his clothes, his beefy fists planted on his hips. They were both staring at the floor and smiling—at Beauty, who was on her belly, inching her way toward Sophia, tail wagging, head cocked to one side, her puppy curiosity clearly wondering, "What sort of chewy treat is this?" Sophia eyeballed the encroaching dog with all the enthusiasm a princess would bestow on week-old stall-muckings.

"Yer about to get yer nose swatted, pup," Baxter warned, his gravelly voice laced with amusement.

No sooner had the words left his mouth than one of Sophia's paws flashed out, catching Beauty's snout. Beauty yelped and tried to scramble away, but she couldn't find her footing on the wood floor and landed on her stomach with her legs splayed. Clearly satisfied that she'd demonstrated who was in charge, Sophia lifted both her tail and her nose in the air, then strolled several feet away to lie down in a pool of sunlight streaming through the window. With the golden rays adoring her, she hoisted a hind leg in the air and proceeded to groom herself.

Relieved that there was no need for concern, Simon stepped into the doorway. Beauty caught sight of him and barked a greeting, then, managing to gain her feet, she darted toward him. Bending down he scooped her up and was instantly the recipient of a wealth of canine adoration, followed by whining that was obviously a report on the terrible fate that had just befallen her. He gave her a sympathetic hug, then holding her in the crook of his arm and dodging doggie kisses as best he could, he entered the kitchen.

His gaze instantly settled on Genevieve. Dressed in

the same demure pale-yellow day gown she'd worn last evening, her blond hair pulled back in a simple chignon, she stole his breath. He stared at her, feeling as if he'd been punched in the heart. Her lips looked ripe and slightly kiss-swollen, yet her beautiful blue eyes offered no indication that the two of them had shared anything more than a casual conversation. That irked him, mainly because he wasn't certain his expression was as inscrutable.

Memories of the previous night flooded his mind... hands and lips exploring, her straddling his thighs, taking him deep into her body, the sound of her moaning his name as she came apart in his arms. Then, holding her close, their limbs entwined, his lips pressed to her temple, breathing in her delicate fragrance. The profound, utter satisfaction that had washed through him— satisfaction, he sensed, that was due to more than mere sexual gratification. He couldn't recall the last time he'd felt so damn good. So damn...content.

Good enough apparently to fall into an uncharacteristically deep sleep. Of course, it had been a long time since he'd been so completely wrung out. Indeed, he couldn't recall a single occasion when he had been so thoroughly exhausted by a woman. Normally he left soon after his passion was spent. Sleeping with a woman, spending the night with her, awakening with her the next morning was too...intimate. Too...serious.

Yet he'd never once thought of leaving that bed. Instead he'd held Genevieve close and fallen into a deep, restful sleep the likes of which he couldn't recall ever experiencing. Until this woman. A woman who was now looking at him with a glimmer of humor in those bewitching blue eyes he couldn't stop staring into.

He cleared his throat. "You're all right?" he asked Genevieve.

"Of course she's all right," Baxter broke in. "I've been watchin' over her while ye slept like a babe. Made her breakfast and tea. Weren't easy considerin' how bare yer pantry is."

Simon shifted his gaze to Baxter, whose glare could have melted bricks. "Obviously you're feeling better."

Baxter grunted. "Good enough to watch over Gen without any help. So now that yer awake, we'll be gettin' ready to leave."

Simon's insides knotted at the words. He couldn't let her go back to the cottage yet, not until he knew what sort of threat she was facing. He realized it was more than that, however. He simply didn't want her to go. Not yet.

He opened his mouth to object, but before he could speak, Genevieve said, "I don't think we should be in such a rush to leave, Baxter. What if whoever attacked you returns?"

Baxter cracked his knuckles. "I'll be ready for him next time."

"Still, I think I'd feel better staying here a while longer. That is, if Simon doesn't object."

"You may both stay as long as you like," Simon assured her. Clearly she suspected the intruder would return. The only reason the bastard would do so was because he hadn't found what he was looking for last night—something he'd discover as soon as he figured out how to open the puzzle box. Simon harbored no doubts that the letter he himself sought was exactly what the intruder was looking for. Genevieve had to know where it was, and based on her reluctance to return to her home, he'd wager it was still somewhere in the cottage.

Yet, if the letter was important enough for her to remove it from the box, why wouldn't she bring it with her? Had she done so? He considered for several seconds, then decided no. She clearly was aware the letter was connected to the break-in—she knew the box was missing. Which meant the letter represented danger. He couldn't see her bringing something like that here, where it could place Baxter in further harm's way. Simon would wager all he owned that the letter remained in her cottage—in whatever fiendishly clever hiding place she'd fashioned for it.

"In fact," he continued, "I think you'd best plan on remaining at least one more night. I also think someone should watch the cottage, in case the man does return."

"I agree, and I volunteer," said Baxter. "I'd like nothin' better than to get my hands on the bastard wot hit me."

"Excellent. I propose you take the day watch, and I'll take the night," Simon said to him. "That way one of us will always be with Genevieve." It was far more likely the intruder would return at night, which would afford Simon hours of uninterrupted time to conduct his own search—a brilliant solution. Besides, Baxter would never agree to leave Genevieve alone with him all night.

Baxter turned to Genevieve. "That agreeable to you?"

She appeared relieved. "Yes, provided you both promise to be very careful."

Baxter nodded then turned back to Simon. "It's agreed. I'll bring home supplies from the cottage when I return this evening so we don't all starve. How have ye not done so already?"

"I've taken my meals in the village. And it's not as if there is no food here. The pantry does contain the basics." Not that he knew how to put them together to actually make something of them. But hell, he was certainly capable of smearing jam and honey on biscuits if he grew hungry between meals.

"Not much more than that." Baxter's gaze flicked to the knife Simon still held. "You plannin' to stab someone?"

"Just a precaution. I wasn't certain you both were safe."

"We're safe, and breakfast is ready." Baxter's gaze raked over Simon, then he crossed his meaty arms over his barrel chest. "I'll wait 'til ye get some clothes on before I leave."

Simon glanced down. He'd completely forgotten his state of undress. "Very well. I'll also pen a note to the magistrate telling him about last night's break-in. I think it best if you deliver it—that way you can give him your personal account of your attack."

Baxter jerked his head in agreement. "I'll visit him before I begin my watch on the cottage."

Thanks to the fire Baxter had built in the hearth, there was hot water. Simon carried a half-filled pail back to his bedchamber with Beauty trotting at his heels. After they entered his room, Beauty promptly began chewing on his boot and he quickly washed, then shaved—an act he was by no means expert at. His valet had never so much as nicked him, a claim Simon couldn't make. But since a steward wouldn't employ a valet, he'd had to learn how to shave himself, and not cut his own throat while doing so.

Twenty minutes later, freshly shaved—with only two nicks—and cleanly dressed—although wearing one boot that bore a row of tooth marks and looked decidedly more worse for the wear than the other—and carrying the note he'd written to the magistrate, he re-entered the kitchen. To his surprise Baxter placed a plate on the table before him along with a cup of tea.

"Best I could do with wot were here," the giant muttered.

"Thank you, Baxter." He tasted the ham, eggs and thinly sliced potatoes and nodded. "Delicious." He was tempted to ask Baxter if he'd started the fire in the hearth with the flames that seemed to shoot from his eyeballs every time he glared at Simon, but as it didn't appear that a sense of humor was one of the giant's better qualities, Simon decided silence was the wiser strategy.

He watched Genevieve as he ate, unable to pull his gaze from where she crouched by the hearth, petting Beauty. Simon noted that she once again wore gloves, and he determined that today would be the day he'd find out why. Beauty flopped onto her back, paws dangling in the air, in a shameless petition for belly-rubbing. Sophia observed the proceedings from the windowsill through narrowed eyes.

Genevieve laughed at Beauty's antics and tickled her gloved fingers over the dog's belly, much to the canine's delight. Simon's own abdomen tingled, recalling the feel of Genevieve's hands exploring him—touching, stroking, caressing, pushing him to the brink of madness. Whatever ailment or injury her hands might suffer from, their touch was pure magic.

As if she felt the weight of his regard, she looked up and their gazes met. Laughter still lurked in her eyes and for several seconds Simon simply couldn't move. Couldn't do anything save stare. Bloody hell, she was lovely. And damn if his heart rate didn't quicken at the prospect of spending the entire day with her.

"I'll be on my way," Baxter said. Simon pulled his gaze away from Genevieve and watched the giant man untie the apron from around his waist. Baxter looked at Genevieve. "Anything I can get for you before I leave?"

"No, thank you. But if you could bring back a fresh gown from the cottage, I'd appreciate it."

"Done." He turned to Simon and scowled. "If any harm comes to her ye'll be answerin' to me. And I can promise ye won't like doin' so." With that he tossed down the apron, snatched up the note Simon had written, and stomped from the room. Seconds later the front door slammed shut.

Simon cleared his throat. "He certainly knows how to make an exit."

"He's very—"

"Protective. Yes, I know. Should I be foolish enough to forget, I'm certain they'll be finding pieces of me all over Little Longstone. I don't believe I've ever met such an...outspoken servant."

A bit of a chill entered her eyes. "That's because he's much more than a servant. He's my friend. More like a brother actually."

"Yes, I can see that." The spy in him—the one concerned with saving his neck from the hangman's noose—coughed to life, demanding he grab the opening she'd so neatly handed him. This was his chance to question her regarding her relationship with Baxter, find out all he could about her. But as it had from the first moment he'd seen her, the man in him, the one who desired her to the point of distraction, won out. He wanted her. Needed her. Now. Everything else could wait.

Setting aside his napkin, he stood and walked toward her, trying to ignore the little voice inside his head chanting *You're alone with her.* She rose as well, her gloved hands lightly clasped in front of her. He halted when less than an arm's length separated them. He tried to resist touching her, if for no other reason than to prove to himself that he could, but he failed utterly. Reaching out, he cupped her face in one palm.

"I was worried when I awoke and discovered you gone."

"Baxter is an early riser, and given last night's occurrence, I knew he'd tap on my door to make certain I was all right. I thought it prudent to return to my own chamber before he did so." Her lips twitched. "Lest we should find pieces of you all over Little Longstone."

"Not to worry. He may outweigh me, but I've a few tricks of my own."

"Yes, I know." Her gaze flicked to his mouth. "You demonstrated them last night."

Bloody hell, she might as well have set a match to him. "Not all of them," he murmured. He brushed the pad of his thumb over her lush lower lip and spoke the simple truth. "It was an incredible night."

"Yes, it was."

"One I'd like to repeat." Another simple truth.

Her gaze searched his for several seconds, then she nodded. "As would I."

He released a breath he hadn't even realized he held. Only a few hours had passed since he'd held her, kissed her, but it suddenly felt like years. And as if he would suffocate if he didn't touch her.

Stepping forward, he erased the distance between them and drew her into his arms. He brushed his mouth over hers, half amused, half irritated that such a feather-light touch ignited him so. Her lips parted and his tongue slipped into the silky heat of her mouth. He felt as if he were sinking into that same dark pool of pleasure in which he'd drowned last night. His hands roamed her back, molding her soft curves to him. Need, hot and urgent, swamped him, vibrating a groan in his throat.

"Genevieve…" Her name came out in a husky rasp as he broke off their kiss to drag his open mouth down the fragrant length of her neck. He wanted her. Now. In the light, where he could see her. Bending his knees, he scooped her up and walked briskly toward his bedchamber.

"Wh-what are you doing?"

"Taking you to bed. Given how badly I want you, I considered the table in the kitchen, but since I've no desire for either of us to suffer splinters in the backside, I'll find the fortitude to wait until we have the comfort of my mattress beneath us. But rest assured, the thirty seconds it's taking us to get there is sorely taxing my patience."

13

EVERYTHING inside Genevieve turned icy with dread. She had to put a stop to this. Immediately. "Simon, please put me down."

"Gladly." He shouldered through the bedchamber door then strode to the bed where he set her down with a gentle bounce. He started to follow her down, but before he could cover her body with his, she rolled away and stood up. She quickly walked to the fireplace, to put as much space as possible between her and his bed. He approached her slowly, his eyes questioning, even more so when she backed away from him. He halted several feet away, and to her vast relief he made no move to touch her again. "I thought you said you wanted more of what we shared last night?"

"Actually, I said I wanted another incredible *night*. And I do." Her gaze shifted briefly to the window where a bright stream of sunlight spilled into the room. "It isn't night."

His gaze searched hers with such intensity, she had the disconcerting sensation he could read her every thought. Finally he said, "You only want to make love in the dark."

"Yes." Although she prayed he'd accept that without any further questions, she knew he wouldn't.

"Why?" To her alarm, he stepped closer, until less than two feet separated them. Her dismay grew when reached out and lightly clasped her shoulders. Dear God, the warmth of his hands felt so good, the heat of them almost melted her resolve. And that could not happen. She could only, would only, give herself to him under the cover of darkness. To do otherwise would only leave her open to rejection.

"Why?" he asked again. "Why would such an exquisite woman insist on hiding herself in the dark?" When she remained silent, he said softly, "This cannot be due to modesty—you're far too passionate."

"Don't you mean wanton?" The words came out more harshly than she'd intended, yet they were true. God knows what he'd think of her if he knew the truth—that she wasn't really a respectable widow, but had spent her entire adult life as a mistress to a nobleman.

A frown creased his brows and he shook his head. "Not if you're attaching any sort of lewd or unsavory connotation to the word, and it sounds as if you are. Please don't tell me you regret what happened between us."

"I don't."

"Good. Because I certainly don't. As for you being wanton…" He touched her face with a tenderness that threatened to undo her. "You are the most exciting, passionate lover I've ever been with. I think you are stunning and I want to see you, all of you, when we make love." He leaned forward and touched his lips to hers. "I want to watch your skin flush and your eyes glaze as you become aroused. Watch as I thrust inside you. Watch you ride me. Watch you come."

Her breath caught at the mental pictures his vivid

words painted. "I want that too, but…I cannot. We must meet in darkness or not at all."

He leaned back and studied her for several long seconds. Then slowly released her. Relief filled her at his acceptance, but it was short-lived, because, rather than stepping away from her as she'd expected, he instead gently clasped her gloved hands and raised them to his chest. She tried to jerk away from him, but he pressed her palms more firmly to him and shook his head. "Your hands are why you don't want to make love without darkness."

It was a statement rather than a question. Anger rushed through her and she had to clamp her lips together to stop herself from snapping out that it was none of his damn concern. She forcefully yanked her hands away from him and stepped back, ignoring the shaft of pain that darted through her fingers. "My reasons are my own."

"Tell me," he said softly. Once again he reached for her hands and to her horror he brought them to his lips and pressed gentle kisses against her gloved palms. His heat branded her skin through the thin kid leather and she gasped. "They felt so good on me last night, touching me, stroking me. Your touch excited me, inflamed me. Pleasured me beyond anything I'd ever experienced. That is something to be celebrated, not hidden. Tell me why you hide them."

Dear God, his persuasive voice, his gentle touch, the warmth of his breath beating through her gloves all conspired to evaporate her resolve. Her anger died as quickly as it had flared, replaced by weary resignation. Clearly he wasn't going to let the matter drop. What difference did it really make if she told him? It wasn't as if their time together wasn't temporary. Telling him didn't mean showing him.

She pulled in a deep breath. "My hands…cause me pain. The condition is called arthritis. My joints swell and become stiff, making it difficult for me to perform certain tasks. I coat them with a special cream that offers me some relief and therefore I wear gloves to keep the cream intact." She didn't add that she hated looking at them, at the daily reminder of why the man she'd been foolish enough to love had cast her aside.

"Do they hurt now?"

"A bit, although not too badly today. It's worse when the weather is damp."

He took her hands and very gently massaged them between his. "Does this help at all?"

"That feels—" *Lovely. Knee-weakeningly so.* "—nice."

"Your hands are why you settled in Little Longstone. To be close to the springs."

She nodded. "They offer me a great deal of relief. The pain started several years ago, just as an occasional twinge, but it grew worse over time, as has the swelling."

"You've seen a doctor?"

"Several. Other than the springs and the cream, they say nothing can be done."

"I'm sorry they cause you pain." Once again he raised her fingers to his lips. "Take off your gloves, Genevieve. Touch me. In the light. I felt your hands on me last night and they were pure magic. Let me see them touching me."

"No." She could barely choke out the word. "I…can't."

"Why? I have a number of scars. I'm hardly perfect."

She snatched her hands away. "Has anyone ever rejected you because of them?" The question came out in a harsh whisper, and to her horror, she felt hot tears push behind her eyes.

He studied her for several long seconds with an expression she couldn't read. Indeed, his only outward sign of emotion was the muscle that ticked in his jaw. "No, but I take it that's what happened to you."

Given her question, her reaction, it would have been ridiculous to deny it. She confirmed his statement with a tight jerk of her head. "My...husband couldn't tolerate ugliness and came to abhor my touch." Her husband, her lover, what did one more lie at this point matter?

Again that muscle in his jaw flexed. "I'm sorry he hurt you. But Genevieve, I'm not him. I'm aching for your touch." He reached out and took one of her hands. Held it between his as if it were a precious treasure. Then slowly, he slid one long finger inside her glove to caress her palm.

She gasped at the intimacy of the gesture. Her mind told her to pull away, but the feel of his finger caressing her, the heat and desire burning in his eyes, rendered her unable to move.

"Beautiful doesn't mean perfect," he said softly, "and there is nothing about you that isn't beautiful. Exquisite. No part of you that I don't want next to me. This is how badly I want you." He grasped her other hand and pressed it to the hard ridge of flesh tenting the front of his breeches. A shiver of pure want rippled through her, and when her fingers involuntarily curved around him, his eyes darkened. "Trust me, Genevieve. Please. If you harbor any fear, it shouldn't be that I'll reject you, but that I'll keep you locked in this room with me for the next fortnight."

She couldn't speak. Could barely breathe. Staring into

his eyes, feeling his arousal pulsing against her palm, his finger stroking her, she couldn't deny him. *Trust me...* She pulled in a shuddering breath, then eased her hands away from him. With her insides quaking, she slowly pulled off her gloves. His gaze never left hers, not until she'd dropped both gloves to the floor. Then she stood before him, fully clothed, yet feeling utterly naked. And more vulnerable than she'd ever felt in her life.

Without looking away from her he pulled his shirt from his breeches then lifted the linen garment over his head and let it fall to the floor. Then he picked up both her hands. Settled them against his chest. Dragged them across his skin.

His eyes slid closed and he let out a long breath. "You cannot know how good that feels." He opened his eyes and her breath halted at the fire burning in their green depths. "Again. Do it again."

Genevieve swallowed and slowly dragged her palms over his skin. He felt hot and hard and his muscles jumped beneath her fingers. He lightly encircled her wrists and pulled her hands away from him and looked down. Genevieve's throat tightened and her every muscle tensed as she braced herself for the passion in his eyes to turn to disgust at the sight of her skin, reddened from the swelling, and the joints that were larger than they should have been.

He studied her hands, gently turning them over. Then, he brought them to his mouth. And gently kissed them.

Genevieve sucked in a harsh breath. "Magic," he whispered against her fingers. "Just like the rest of you." He drew the tip of her index finger into his mouth and slowly swirled his tongue around it before letting it free. "Delicious. Just like the rest of you." He pressed her palm to his cheek. "Beautiful. Just like the rest of you."

A sob welled in Genevieve's throat, one that escaped her in a trio of jerky sounds when Simon turned his head and kissed her palm. His words, the sight of his mouth against her imperfect hand, pleasures she'd never thought to experience again, simply undid her. The dam inside her burst, releasing the moisture that pushed behind her eyes. Tears overflowed, dripping down her cheeks, wetting their joined hands. Without a word he pulled her into his arms and settled his mouth on hers, coaxing her with feather-light kisses. Her shivers turned into shudders of delight and with a moan she parted her lips. He kissed her with a slow exploration that made it seem as if he had hours to do so, and his very leisurely approach filled her with impatience. Desperate urgency filled her and she pressed herself more closely against him. Her skin felt tight and hot, as if it had shrunk. She tangled her fingers in his silky hair and leaned back far enough to whisper against his lips, "I want to see all of you, Simon. Touch all of you. Now. Please, *now.*"

Breathing heavily, he stepped back and quickly dispensed with the rest of his clothes. When he stood before her, hair disheveled from her impatient fingers, eyes glittering with desire, arousal jutting, a thrill of feminine pleasure raced through her. She reached out and stroked his erection, immensely satisfied not only by his groan, but by the pearls of fluid that leaked from the engorged tip. She painted the wetness over him, stroking his length with one hand while the other slipped between his legs to cup him, all while reveling in the sight of his avid gaze watching her touch him.

"I'm not going to be able to stand much more of that," he said, slowly thrusting into her hand.

"Neither am I." Her sex throbbed with need, her own slick wetness coating her folds.

Her words clearly inflamed him. He looked as if he wanted to swallow her in one gulp, a look that fired her every nerve-ending into burning awareness. With a growl rumbling in his throat, he grabbed her bodice and yanked it down along with her chemise. While he pushed the garments over her hips, she kicked off her shoes. When nothing remained except her garters and stockings, he simply lifted her against him and, with his lips claiming hers, walked to the bed, her feet dangling several inches off the floor.

He sat on the mattress then lay back, taking her with him. Her body covered his, his erection trapped between them, the hard ridge of flesh searing her. His fingers tunneled through her hair, scattering pins, until long strands surrounded them like a curtain. He looked up at her, his eyes intense, filled with need. "Ride me."

Genevieve's heart stuttered at the hoarse command. She straddled his hips, taking him into her body in a slow, deep, wet impalement that dragged a ragged groan from her throat. Setting her hands on his chest, she slowly rocked against him, lifting up until only the head of his erection remained in her, then sliding down again, loving the way he watched her body swallow him.

He let her set the pace, and at first she kept her movements slow, luxuriating in sensual sensation. The delicious feel of his length stretching her, the musky scent of her arousal mingling with his. The sound of his harsh breathing enraptured her. And most miraculous of all, she gazed in awe at the sight of her hands skimming over his muscular chest, her fingers sifting through the smattering of ebony curls darkening his skin.

His strong hands cupped her breasts, teasing the hard points of her nipples, each tug of his fingers shooting exquisite shards of sensation straight to her womb. She threw her head back, saturated in pleasure, her movements quickening, her orgasm a whisper away, a whisper that evaporated when he slipped one hand down her torso, to tangle in the curls between her legs and circle her clitoris. Her climax hit her like a bolt of lightning. She cried out as spasms of pleasure gripped her. Beneath her Simon tensed, her name a guttural groan on his lips as his release pulsed inside her.

With tiny aftershocks still rippling through her, Genevieve melted against Simon's chest and buried her face against his neck. At least a minute passed before she could raise her head. When she did, she found him staring at her, as if he'd been waiting for her to look at him. His gaze probed hers, intense, as if searching for something.

Tucking a curl behind her ear, he said, "Thank you."

She shook her head. "No, thank *you*."

His fingertips traced her eyebrows. "For what?"

She wished she could keep her answer light and breezy, along the lines of "for the very enjoyable romp and much-appreciated orgasm," but she couldn't. "For giving me back something I thought I'd lost forever. For not finding fault. For…accepting. And finding beauty where there is none."

"'Beauty is bought by judgment of the eye,'" he quoted.

"Shakespeare," she murmured. *"Love's Labours Lost."*

"Yes. Where you find no beauty, I judge there to be an abundance."

His words made the space around her heart go hollow, an unsettling sensation she shoved aside to be examined at another time. "Thank you," she said softly, then asked, "Why did *you* thank *me?*"

Something flickered in his eyes, something she couldn't decipher other than to know it looked troubled. It disappeared as quickly as it came, leaving her wondering if she'd imagined it. "For telling me the truth. For trusting me."

Guilt slapped Genevieve, and she leaned down to brush her lips over his so he couldn't see her eyes. Because, while she'd told him the truth about her hands, she'd lied to him about a great deal more. And for the first time in a very long while, her conscience pricked her for being less than truthful.

When she was certain her lies wouldn't show in her eyes, she lifted her head and offered him a smile. "You're welcome. And now that I've had my wicked way with you, how do you propose we spend the rest of the day?"

His hands slowly smoothed down her back to cup her bottom. "I can think of half a dozen things we could do."

She cocked a brow. "Half a dozen? That's quite a few."

"And that's without even trying." He leaned up to kiss her. "And before luncheon."

"Oh, my. But I thought your pantry was bare."

"There are biscuits. And jam. And honey."

"It just so happens I'm very fond of biscuits. And jam. And honey."

His smile could have melted the soles of her shoes, had she been wearing any. "I don't know when I've heard better news. I think honey would go well right here." He drew a lazy fingertip around one of her nipples then dipped his head to lave the sensitive peak with his tongue.

"To start," she murmured. And with that he rolled them over, and the magic began all over again.

14

THE SUN was close to setting, the autumn sky streaked with fiery fingers of red and gold, when Simon and Genevieve, pulled along by an energetic Beauty, neared the path that led to his cottage. Simon deliberately slowed their footsteps, knowing that very soon Baxter would be returning from Genevieve's home and their day together would be over. And he wasn't ready for it to end.

For the past quarter-hour, as they'd strolled along the wooded path from the springs after Genevieve had soaked her hands, he'd tried his damnedest to recall the last time he'd spent such an enjoyable day, only to finally conclude that he never had.

How was that possible? How could it be that in nearly thirty years of living—a life filled with privilege, friendships, lovers, parties, passion and adventure—that this day, with this woman, out of all the days he could recall from a lifetime of days, was his favorite? He didn't know, but there was no denying it.

They'd spent hours in sensual exploration, their bouts of lovemaking interspersed with laughter, conversation and a picnic of biscuits, jam and honey on the hearth rug in his bedchamber—a meal that led to an even more delicious pastime of painting honey on each others' bodies. After licking off the sweetness, they'd made love again, their skins warmed by the fire and bathed in flickering golden light. Genevieve was not only beautiful, she was witty and intelligent and an exciting, adventurous and generous lover. He'd found himself unable to stop touching her, and was consumed with the unprecedented desire to wrap his arms around her and never let go, to meld their bodies so tightly together they couldn't be separated.

There were women he'd known for years with whom he didn't feel so comfortable, with whom he didn't share such an easy rapport. And never had there been one who set his blood on fire as Genevieve did. Every minute spent in her company only served to further convince him that she hadn't been, in any way, involved in Ridgemoor's death. Indeed, he was convinced she didn't even know her former lover was dead. Surely a woman who'd trusted him enough to remove those gloves, to show him, share with him that which she considered her greatest shame, was trustworthy. He'd asked her to trust him, and although she had no real reason to, she had.

And damn it, that kicked at his conscience—a fact that both unsettled and alarmed him. It had never bothered him in the past to coax confidences from people while feeding them a sack of lies. It was all part of his work. After all, he could hardly announce to suspects, "Good afternoon, I'm a spy for the British Crown, come to unearth all your secrets. But if you'd simply tell them to me, it would save me a great deal of time and trouble."

Yet because he was not telling her who he was, why he was here, each lie was beginning to taste like a dose of bitter medicine. Which could only mean that the stirrings of discontent he'd experienced over the past months were more pressing than he'd believed. If he couldn't stomach telling lies, then his days as a spy were truly numbered. Indeed more than once today he'd considered telling her the truth, but his mind warned him to be cautious, that he didn't really know her, that while she'd shared one secret with him, she had others—the fact that she'd been a mistress, and her secret identity as Charles Brightmore. But his heart…his heart which had never before been so engaged told him her secrets regarding her past were only to protect herself and her reputation in Little Longstone. They were not for any nefarious reasons.

This day in her company had also convinced him that Ridgemoor had been a bloody, blind fool. He knew that when Genevieve claimed her husband had rejected her, she had really meant that it had been Ridgemoor who had done so. He frowned at the earl's idiocy, and anger pumped through him for the way Ridgemoor had hurt her. He'd never forget the trepidation in her eyes, the vulnerability when she'd removed her gloves, so brave, yet so fearful that he'd reject her. That any man could do something like that simply stunned him. These hours in her company had left him with a deep hunger for more. More days like this.

"Heavens, what a frown you're sporting," Genevieve said, her voice pulling him from his brown study. "That scowl doesn't bode well for whomever you're contemplating."

Simon relaxed his features and offered her a smile. "Actually I was thinking about you."

"Oh, dear. It couldn't have been good."

"On the contrary, it was very good."

"Your forbidding expression says otherwise."

"It was due to my inability to come up with the correct word. I was thinking how enjoyable this day has been, only to realize that *enjoyable* is much too lukewarm a word to describe it." Beauty stopped to sniff at a tuft of dried grass and Simon turned to face Genevieve. "It's been…"

"So much better than merely enjoyable?" she suggested with a half smile.

"Yes." He lifted her hand—her ungloved hand—to his lips and pressed a kiss against her fingers. "It's been the sort of day I'd like very much to repeat."

His hope that she'd echo the sentiment withered and died when her warm amusement faded, replaced by unmistakable chagrin. Everything inside him froze with disappointment. Damn. Clearly she hadn't found the day as special as he had, although this was the first indication of that.

It was only with the greatest effort that he managed to keep his expression neutral. When she said nothing, simply continued to stare at him with those dismay-filled eyes, he finally spoke the obvious truth that hovered between them like a dark cloud. "You don't want the same thing." The words came out flatly, which was fitting as flattened was precisely how he felt.

Even more dismay filled her eyes and she shook her head. "That's not true. I do. It's just…" She stepped away and paced several times before turning to face him. She lifted her chin and met his gaze squarely. "I'm afraid I haven't been entirely honest with you, Simon. And if we're to spend more time together…see each other again as we have today, then I'd prefer it to be without lies between us."

His conscience slapped him for his own dishonesty, a blow he forced himself to ignore. "I'm listening." When she hesitated, he said softly, "Genevieve, I give you my word that whatever you tell me will remain just between us."

"Thank you." She swallowed, then spoke, the words coming out in a rush. "My circumstances are not what I led you to believe. The truth is, I am not a widow. Indeed, I've never been married. For ten years I was the mistress of a nobleman, a man whose mistress I would still be if he hadn't terminated our arrangement last year when he could no longer stand to have my less-than-perfect hands touch him. For the sake of propriety and discretion, I've presented myself as a widow." She paused, moistened her lips, then lifted her chin another notch. "I realize you will probably now think ill of me—"

He stopped her words with a fingertip to her lips. "I don't think ill of you at all, Genevieve." Bloody hell, he wished he did, for surely that would be preferable to this unsettling, uncharacteristic possessiveness sweeping through him, one that filled him with the overwhelming urge to protect her from anyone or anything that might hurt her. "Your deception is completely understandable given the circumstances. I appreciate your honesty." Yes, even though it lodged a tight ball of guilt in his gut.

Some of the tension drained from her expression. He moved his hand from her lips to lightly brush his fingers over her soft cheek. "How did you come to be his mistress?" He knew he had no right to ask, but damn it, he wanted to know just the same.

Long seconds passed and he could see she struggled with what and how much to reveal. Finally she said quietly, "My mother was a prostitute. She wanted more for me. Didn't want me to suffer the sort of life she'd endured, and God knows I wanted more for myself. Unfortunately, women have very few choices." Her lips tightened. "She saved every shilling she could so I wouldn't have to become what she was. I had an aptitude for drawing and painting and she bought me supplies. When I was fifteen we came to London and she went to work in a brothel. I worked there as well—as the seamstress, cook and laundress. That's where I met Baxter. I found him in the alley behind the brothel one winter morning. He'd been beaten and left for dead. I brought him to my room and by some miracle, he survived."

Simon's insides knotted. Bloody hell, at fifteen he'd enjoyed every privilege his family's rank and wealth had afforded, while Genevieve and Baxter had been fighting to survive. He cleared his throat. "You saved his life. No wonder he is so protective of you."

"And I of him. He returned the favor by becoming the brother I never had." She drew a deep breath, then continued, "I continued my work, and painted in what little spare time I had. Claudia, the madam, liked my work and displayed my paintings in the house, which filled me with the foolish hope that someday I might become a real artist. Unfortunately, Claudia died, and under the new madam, the situation at the house, as well as the clientele, began to change. My mother was beaten several times by clients and I was desperate to get her— both of us—out."

A bitter sound escaped her. "Sadly, there weren't many places we could go, especially places where I could simply work in the kitchen and laundry and not render sexual favors. To make matters worse, the new madam claimed my mother owed her money for the wages she'd lost when she couldn't work while recuperating from her beatings. She wouldn't consider letting Mother go until the debt was paid and the interest she levied was exorbitant. Although I hated to leave my mother alone there, I sought a position as a governess, but it quickly became clear that the man of the house expected me to entertain him once his wife and the children were abed. I was desperate enough to do it, to do anything to earn enough of a wage to get my mother out of that house and not have her forced to lift her skirts in back alleys at the docks. I was prepared to give in, to do what was necessary, when my mother called upon me at the house where I was employed. She told me that during the several weeks I'd been gone, she'd met a man…a kind man, a wealthy man who was a regular of one of the other girls. A man who'd admired one of my paintings. When my mother told him her daughter had painted it, he said he wished to meet me."

"And that was the nobleman."

She nodded. "I found him handsome and agreeable, kind and, most importantly at that point, very generous. Being with him saved me from my repulsive employer and enabled me to remove my mother from her horrid situation."

"So you saved her as well."

Unmistakable sorrow shadowed her eyes and she shook her head. "She died less than a year later. But at least I have the solace of knowing her final months were as comfortable as possible."

"Did you love him?" Another question he had no right to ask, but he wanted the answer just the same.

"Not at first. But over time…yes, I grew to love

him. He was very good to me. Until..." Her voice trailed off and her gaze dropped to her hands. "Until he stopped caring."

"Do you ever see him?"

Something flickered in her eyes then she shook her head. "No. Nor do I expect to. He made it perfectly clear that he wanted no more to do with me, that our arrangement was irrevocably severed."

Yes. Until he'd sent her the puzzle box. "Do you still love him?"

She considered, then said, "No, he effectively snuffed out that flame, although I will always be grateful for the protection he gave me, and for making it possible to help my mother. It turned out that the man I loved did not really exist—if he had, he would not have cast me aside. Yet even as I say that, I do not blame him for doing so."

Simon barely managed to tamp down his anger. "You *should* blame him. His reason for abandoning you was dishonorable and selfish in the extreme."

A humorless sound passed her lips. "I'm flattered by your outrage on my behalf, but truly, what good is a mistress if she no longer brings pleasure?"

"Any man who didn't find you immeasurably pleasurable is blind. And a complete arse." Her words, her manner, all cemented what he'd already known in his heart—she didn't know Ridgemoor was dead.

Her eyes went soft, like a summer sky blurred by a gentle rain, and she gave him a tremulous smile. "Thank you."

"What of your painting?"

"I enjoyed it for many years, but it would be too difficult now." Her gaze flicked to her hands.

"Have you tried?"

"No. Not recently. I was afraid…"

"Afraid of what?"

"Failing. Of not being able to create anything beautiful again." A frown creased her brow. "But now… you've given me hope that…" Her expression cleared and she gazed into his eyes. "Well, perhaps I'll try it again."

"I think you should. And I hope you do." A memory flashed through his mind and realization hit him. "The painting in your sitting room, above the fireplace. That's your work."

She nodded. "Yes. It was always my favorite."

"I can understand why. It's extraordinary." *Just like you.*

"Thank you. Simon, I want you to know…he was the only man I was ever with. Until now. Until you."

Bloody hell, he felt as if his heart shifted in his chest. "Thank you for telling me. I know it cannot have been easy to share something so deeply personal."

"You're welcome." Her gaze searched his, and once again he could see the vulnerability in her eyes. "And now that you know the truth…is today still the sort of day you'd like very much to repeat?"

"Yes," he said without hesitation. "You?"

"Yes."

Her smile damn near undid him, and he cursed the fact that for today, at least, their time was nearly over. She glanced down and he followed her gaze, noting that Beauty had fallen asleep with her head resting on his boot.

"We've bored the dog to sleep," she said.

"Good. Otherwise she'd be wanting to gallop down the path and I wouldn't be able to do this." He drew her into his arms and brushed his lips over hers. She immediately opened for him, and with a groan he sank into the kiss, his tongue exploring the silky heat of her mouth. And he prayed they would have the opportunity to enjoy another day like this before his mission and his life in London separated them.

15

SIMON STOOD in Genevieve's sitting room and stared at the painting hung over the mantel, the painting she had created. He lifted the single candle he held, noting again the vibrant colors that seemed to jump off the canvas even in the dim light. The intriguing brush strokes. The vividness of the sea waves that were so lifelike he could almost hear them smashing against the cliffs. Was the blond woman gazing out over the water Genevieve? He found himself reaching out to touch the lone figure. In addition to her intelligence, wit, kindness, charm, beauty and sensuality, she was immensely talented. Or had been, until the problem with her hands had stolen her confidence.

With a sigh, he forced his attention back to the matter at hand and moved about the room, searching for hidden recesses in the paneling, loose bricks in the fireplace, false bottoms in the desk drawers, loose floorboards—anything that might provide a hiding place for the letter he sought, all the while fighting his frustration over the fact that he was no closer to knowing who had killed Ridgemoor than when he'd arrived in Little Longstone. Simon considered sending Waverly a message, asking if he or Miller or Albury had discovered anything that could clear his name, but he quickly discarded the idea.

A message could be intercepted, and Simon wasn't
ready for his whereabouts to be known. He was certain
a political foe of Ridgemoor's had killed him, but which
one? There were dozens. And Simon was running out
of time. Damn it, he needed that letter.

He moved methodically through each room, concentrating on his task, but when he searched Genevieve's
bedchamber, his gaze kept straying to her bed, his imagination filled with flashing images of the two of them,
limbs entwined, hands and lips exploring, bodies
arching. He squeezed his eyes shut to banish the erotic
mental pictures, but that only rendered them more
intense. Muttering an obscenity, he purposefully shifted
to face away from the bed and turned his attention to the
escritoire.

After a thorough examination of the small desk failed
to yield the letter, he once again opened the top drawer.
His hands lingered over the handwritten pages of what
he didn't doubt was a sequel to the *Ladies' Guide.* His
fingers traced the tight, painstaking script, his heart
squeezing in sympathy at how painful it was for her to
write. It was fortunate she'd found this place, Little
Longstone, where she had access to the hot spring that
brought her relief. It was where she belonged. While his
life was in London. Where he belonged.

His gaze dropped to a woven basket next to the desk
and he bent down to retrieve a crumpled piece of paper
from within. He flattened the square sheet and peered
at the words, written in Genevieve's hand.

Today's Modern Woman must always keep her
head about her when in the company of a charming,
attractive gentleman. The more charming and

attractive the man, the more difficult this is to accomplish, therefore concentrating on something unrelated to him, such as mentally reciting Hamlet's soliloquy, or something tedious such as counting to one hundred can prove very useful.

A small smile tugged at his lip at the advice. She was a remarkably insightful woman. The last line was badly smudged, no doubt the reason she'd tossed the sheet away. For reasons he couldn't explain, other than to know he couldn't throw that bit of her back into the trash, he folded the paper and tucked it into his waistcoat pocket, then continued his search.

Several hours later, just before the first streaks of dawn leaked through the darkness to paint the sky, he finished the last room and heaved a heavy sigh. He'd found nothing—except his suddenly active conscience, which had balked incessantly at invading Genevieve's privacy.

Damn it, he should have just asked her what had become of the letter. He should have confided in her, as she had him. Confessed who he was. Why he was in Little Longstone. Of course, then he'd have had to confess he'd spied on her. Searched her home. And he didn't doubt for a minute that she'd believe the only reason he'd sought her out, had flirted with her had been to gain her confidence.

And she would be correct.

But what had started out as nothing more than a calculated scheme to relieve her of the letter had turned into much more. By the time he'd seduced her, his mission had all but been forgotten. He'd believed himself capable of bedding her simply for his mission, but in the end, the mission hadn't played any part in his making love to her. But would she believe that? Bloody hell, he didn't know. But regardless, he was going to have to ask her for the letter, since he couldn't find it on his own. Then, he'd have to pray she'd give it to him...and that she'd forgive him his lies.

A frown crossed his face. Once he left Little Longstone he'd never see her again, so it didn't really matter if she forgave him or not.

Did it?

It matters, his inner voice whispered. And he realized with a jolt that it did. It mattered a whole bloody lot. Which was a whole bloody lot more than it should have mattered.

With a sigh, he blew out his candle and headed for the foyer. Might as well walk around the outside of the house, see if anything was afoot. Maybe the brisk air would clear his head. He entered the foyer and reached for the doorknob.

"Don't move, or I'll shoot a hole through you" came a deep voice from the shadows behind him.

Simon froze and inwardly cursed for allowing himself to be caught unawares. The voice came from nearby, close enough for Simon to know he'd never survive the gunshot wound if the intruder's aim was even partially accurate, yet far enough away that he didn't like his chances of rushing the stranger with the hopes of disarming him. His best alternative was to do as he was told. For now.

"I'm not moving," Simon assured him.

"Put your hands behind your head, nice and slow. A quick move will earn you a lead ball in the back."

Everything in Simon froze as recognition hit him. That voice...bloody hell, he knew that voice. He wished its familiarity filled him with relief, but instead a cold stone of dread landed in his stomach. "You have the wrong person," he said, slowly raising his hands, stalling for time, hoping that the horrible realization forming in his mind wasn't true. Yet he knew in his gut that it was. And that behind him stood not only Ridgemoor's murderer but the man who'd betrayed Simon, and far worse, his country.

"You're the right person, Kilburn. Sadly for you, you're in the wrong place."

In a tone that belied the fury and sickening betrayal racing through him, Simon said, "Not the warmest greeting for an old friend, Waverly."

Behind him, John Waverly, his superior, his mentor, a man he'd trusted and respected above all others, gave a humorless laugh. "We aren't friends, Kilburn."

Feeling as if he'd been gutted, Simon turned around. "Yes, that seems evident."

"I told you not to move."

"Yes, I know, but you needed me to turn around. A man can hardly shoot himself in the back, and I'm assuming that's your plan—to shoot me, then place the gun in my lifeless hand to make it look as if I killed myself."

"Over guilt for betraying your country and killing Ridgemoor," Waverly agreed, as if they were discussing the weather. "Your suicide note will explain everything."

"No one will believe that," Simon said, wishing it were true, but knowing that it wasn't. Forging a convincing note in Simon's handwriting wouldn't present a problem for a man of Waverly's skills.

"Yes, they will." Waverly stepped forward, his pistol aimed at Simon's head, right where someone committing suicide would shoot. Waverly was an expert shot, but even if he wasn't, it would be difficult to miss his target at such close range. Simon would be dead before he hit the floor.

"Murdering Ridgemoor wasn't necessary, John."

"I'm afraid it was. The possibility of him becoming the next prime minister was growing every day. His radical reforms would have ruined a number of very profitable enterprises for me. I have my finger in pies all over London. You'd be amazed at what a tidy sum I pull in from those workhouses alone. That bleeding heart, Ridgemoor, wanted to put an end to all that. All I needed was a few more years and I could have left the spy game an extremely wealthy man."

Rage churned in Simon's stomach. "From money gained by the suffering of others, suffering Ridgemoor wanted to see cease."

Waverly shrugged. "Everyone suffers. Except perhaps people like you, those born to wealth and privilege. But neither your wealth nor your title will prevent you from suffering now, although I suppose you should thank me for ensuring that your end will be quick."

"My gratitude knows no bounds."

Waverly shook his head and made a *tsk*ing sound. "Sarcasm doesn't become you, Simon."

"Ridgemoor might not have become prime minister."

"It didn't matter. Even without gaining that position, he was far too influential. His suspicions of me were enough to make his elimination necessary. Unfortunately my first attempt on his life failed. When he confronted me, told me he not only had proof of my illegal activities, but that it was me who'd tried to kill him, his fate was sealed."

"Proof he'd written in a letter."

Waverly nodded. "Yes. Very annoying of him. In

spite of my strong encouragement, he refused to tell me where the letter was. You were due to arrive at any moment and therefore I couldn't afford to spend any more time with him. I'd convinced myself he was bluffing—until you came to me with your request for two weeks to prove your innocence. I knew the only way you could do so would be with that letter, that Ridgemoor must have been alive when you arrived and have told you about it."

"So you followed me here."

"Yes." He made a disgusted sound. "I should have known he'd send the letter off to his whore for safekeeping."

Simon's every muscle tensed. "Mrs. Ralston knows nothing about this."

"I disagree. She knows enough to have removed the letter from the puzzle box."

Bloody hell. It was Waverly's presence he'd sensed at the festival. Waverly who'd broken into Genevieve's home and attacked Baxter. Simon's stomach stopped churning and tightened into a knot. Unless he could convince Waverly Genevieve had no knowledge of the letter's content, he knew the man would kill her. Before he could speak, Waverly said, "Don't deny it, Kilburn. If you'd removed the letter, you wouldn't still be here searching for it."

"She did find the letter in the box," Simon confirmed, "but she doesn't know what the letter says."

"If you're trying to tell me she cannot read—"

"She can read, but Ridgemoor wrote it in code," Simon improvised, although he suspected it was indeed true—Ridgemoor was an intelligent and cautious man. "She has no idea of the information it contains. It would read as nothing more than harmless words on the page to her."

Waverly's lips curved into an unpleasant smile. "Well, then. It will be a pleasure to convince her to turn the letter over to me."

Simon swallowed the growl of icy rage that rushed into his throat. The thought of this monster going anywhere near Genevieve filled him with a dark violence he'd never before known. "She doesn't have it. I do."

Waverly's smile vanished and his eyes narrowed to slits. "You're lying. You've moved her into your house, and she's now your whore instead of Ridgemoor's. Clearly you'd say anything to protect her."

It was true—he would say anything, do anything to ensure her safety. Swallowing the acid burning in his throat, he shrugged. "Your attack on her manservant provided an excellent excuse for me to get them both away from here, allowing me the freedom to search for the letter." He paused, then added, "And I found it."

Waverly studied him for several seconds. "Where is it?"

"In my waistcoat pocket."

A combination of doubt and greed flickered in Waverly's eyes. "Where did you find it?"

"The sitting room. Hidden behind a loose brick in the fireplace."

Waverly's shook his head. "You're lying. I examined that fireplace and found nothing."

Again Simon shrugged. "You didn't have the time I did to devote to the task and the hiding place was easy to miss. I'd be delighted to show you the spot if you'd like."

"Just give me the letter."

"You told me not to move."

Annoyance tightened Waverly's expression. "Don't

play games with me, Kilburn. I could just shoot you then retrieve the letter from your pocket myself."

"You could…but you don't want to kill me until you know that I really have it. Because if I'm lying and I don't, well, then I'd be dead and unable to tell you where it is."

Waverly's eyes went flat. "You'll slowly reach one hand into your pocket and withdraw the letter. If you've lied to me not only will I shoot you, but I'll see to it that your brother and sister don't live long enough to attend your funeral."

Waverly's hand holding the pistol was perfectly steady and Simon knew his aim would be true. And that meant he had one only chance, one split second to save Genevieve and his family. Cold calm settled over him. He doubted he'd walk away from this alive, but he damn well intended to make sure Waverly didn't either.

With his gaze locked on Waverly's, Simon slowly reached into his waistcoat pocket and withdrew the folded piece of paper he'd taken from Genevieve's bed-chamber. Waverly's eyes glittered and shifted to the letter. The hint of a self-satisfied smile whispered over his lips. Simon held out the paper. Then dropped it.

Waverly's gaze followed the paper and Simon didn't hesitate. *One chance. One chance.* With lightning speed he crouched down, slipped the knife from his boot, and let it fly. Waverly's howl of rage was immediately followed by the deafening report of his pistol. Searing pain suffused Simon. He fell backwards and the world went black.

16

"HURRY, Baxter," Genevieve urged as she made her way down the path. Her cottage was just around the curve and she quickened her stride, tension and unease gripping her increasingly with every step. The first mauve streaks of dawn had lightened the sky more than half an hour ago, more than enough time for Simon to have returned home. The fact that he hadn't twisted her insides with dread.

"More than likely he just lost track of time," Baxter muttered. "Or—and I hate to say this to ye—but be prepared for the fact that he's taken off, Gen. Wouldn't be the first scoundrel to run from a woman after gettin' what he wanted from her."

Genevieve shook her head. "No. He wouldn't do that. He's not like that." She knew it. In her heart. No man who'd looked at her the way he had, made love to her as he had, touched her, kissed her hands as he had, with complete acceptance—that was not a man who would toss her aside, especially without so much as a goodbye.

"Bloody hell, Gen, *all* men are like that."

"Not all. You're not."

"That's 'cause I ain't lookin' to bed ye. I'll tell ye this—even though I think yer better off without him, if that bastard's left without so much as a fare-thee-well, I'll hunt him down and make him sorry he were ever born."

"Baxter, you—"

Her words chopped off when the sound of a pistol shot rent the air. She froze and for several shocked heartbeats her mind went blank. Then a single word screamed through her brain. *Simon.*

Before she could pull a breath into her stalled lungs, Baxter wrapped a hand around her upper arm and jerked her off the path and behind a tree.

"That came from just ahead," he whispered, unsheathing his knife.

Genevieve moistened her dry lips. "Yes. From the cottage. Where Simon is. And as far as I know, he doesn't carry a pistol." With icy fingers of fear clutching her, she slipped her own pistol from the pocket of her pelisse. When she stepped forward, Baxter blocked her with an outstretched arm. "You stay here," he whispered with a frown. "I'll check things out."

"I'm going with you." When his frown deepened, she glared right back at him and repeated, "I'm going with you."

He muttered something about willful women, then keeping to the shadows, he led the way to the cottage. They approached cautiously, surveying the area, but couldn't find anything amiss. Until they opened the door.

Genevieve's heart stalled at the sight of Simon sprawled on the foyer floor, the scarlet puddle surrounding his head widening as blood oozed from his temple. Another man Genevieve had never seen before lay on the other side of the foyer, a knife she recognized as Simon's protruding from his chest.

"Dear God." She ran to Simon's side and dropped to her knees. The bitter, metallic scent of his blood, the sight of it leaking from that ghastly wound, filled her with a terror she'd never before known, terror that threatened to paralyze her. Dragging in a ragged breath, she gave herself a mental slap and tore off her pelisse. Later. She could panic later. She wadded the end of the garment into a makeshift compress which she pressed against the wound with one unsteady hand while her other hand touched Simon's neck and sought out his pulse. And she prayed she'd feel it.

"This bloke is dead," Baxter reported from behind her. She heard him rise and approach her. "How is Cooper?"

She located Simon's pulse and she nearly swooned with relief when she felt the faint, irregular throb beneath her fingertips. "Alive. Bring water, compresses and bandages. And Baxter…" She tore her gaze away from Simon to look up. "Please hurry."

He took off at a run down the corridor toward the kitchen, and Genevieve pulled in another shuddering breath. "Simon, can you hear me? It's Genevieve," she said in voice that trembled with the fear racing through her. A lump swelled in her throat and she forced herself to swallow the sob trapped there. "Please wake up, Simon."

His blood soaked through the compress with frightening speed, wetting her palm, and she quickly folded over another layer of her pelisse, cursing the stiffness in her hands that slowed her actions. She applied as much pressure to the wound as she could then leaned over him to touch her forehead to his.

"Please, Simon. My darling Simon…you must wake up. If you do, I'll have Baxter bake you an entire tray of scones. Or a pie. I know how you harbor a weakness for sweets…"

He didn't move. Didn't make a sound. She straightened and folded over another compress, fighting back her alarm at the amount of blood still welling from the wound. She pressed tighter, prayed harder, and again leaned down to feel his shallow breaths feathering across her cheek.

This was all her fault. This never would have happened if he hadn't been trying to protect her. If she hadn't accepted that box from Richard. Clearly the letter was what the dead man had been after—what other reason could there be? She should have sent the damnable box right back. Because she hadn't, Baxter had been injured, and now Simon...God, Simon might die.

"Don't leave me," she whispered, terrified at his chalky pallor. "Please don't leave me. I just found you. I cannot bear to lose you. I cannot lose another man I love."

The realization, the irrefutable knowledge, that she loved him filled her with wretched despair and a half sob escaped her. She'd never thought she'd fall in love again. And certainly not so hard. Or so quickly. And definitely not with a man who was bleeding to death before her eyes.

Dear God, what she felt for Simon made her feelings for Richard pale in comparison. How could that be? She didn't know, but there was no denying it. And the thought of losing him before she could tell him...no. *No.* She couldn't allow that to happen.

She put her lips next to his ear and whispered, "I love you, Simon. Please wake up so I can tell you. Please..."

Baxter returned and they worked together in silence, Genevieve preparing compresses, Baxter applying pressure to the wound. She gently wiped the blood from Simon's face and neck, her anxious gaze searching for any sign of consciousness, her fingers locating his pulse again to assure herself he still lived.

She didn't know how many terrifying minutes had

passed since they'd entered the foyer. Surely it hadn't been more than five or six, yet it felt like an eternity. Just when she didn't think she could stand another instant of silence, Baxter reported, "The bleeding's nearly stopped. He's got a hell of an egg on his head—but nothing else. Looks like he were just grazed."

No sooner had he said the words than Simon gave a faint groan. Genevieve's gaze flew to his face. His eyelids fluttered, then slowly blinked open. She clasped his hand between hers, pressing it to her chest, just above the spot where her heart beat in frantic thumps.

"Simon, can you hear me?" she asked.

He blinked several times and Genevieve bit back the cry of relief that rushed into her throat when his green gaze met hers. He slowly moistened his lips. "Are you all right?"

She couldn't suppress her half sob, half laugh at his whispered question. Gripping his hand tighter, she brought it to her lips. "Yes, I'm fine." An outright lie—she was sick with worry, lightheaded with relief, and more frightened than she'd ever been in her life. Without turning away from Simon, she said, "I can handle things here now, Baxter. Please fetch Dr. Bailey. And the magistrate."

Baxter nodded. "I'll just check the house first," he said, and then immediately went to do so. As soon as they were alone, Simon whispered, "Genevieve."

"I'm right here, Simon."

He frowned, then winced. "Bloody hell, my head feels like it's been split open. What happened?"

"You were shot."

He blinked again, then tried to move. He sucked in a hissing breath, slammed his eyes shut and went still. After several slow, deep breaths, he said through gritted teeth, "Waverly?"

"I'm guessing that's the name of the man who shot you."

She watched his entire body tense. He tried to nod and clearly thought better of it. "Yes. Is he—"

"He's dead, Simon," she said in a soothing tone. She gently brushed back a lock of hair from his forehead, a dark slash against his frighteningly pale skin.

That news seemed to relax him. "Good."

Baxter entered the foyer. "All's clear. I'll be back with the doctor and the magistrate." He departed, closing the door behind him.

Simon pulled in a few more breaths, then asked, "How did you find me?"

"When you didn't return at sunrise, Baxter and I were worried. We came here and found you bleeding and unconscious, and the other man dead, with your knife sticking out of his chest."

Simon kept his eyes closed and waited for the room to stop spinning and for the thunderous pounding in his head and the nausea roiling through his stomach to subside. After several slow, careful breaths, he again opened his eyes and saw Genevieve. The worry clouding her beautiful features filled him with guilt—and dread. He harbored no doubts that after he had told her what he must, all that caring and concern would fade from her gaze.

"Can you tell me what happened?" she asked.

With the nausea gone and the pounding in his head lessened to a dull roar, he nodded, then moved to sit up. Even with Genevieve's assistance, the going was slow and the effort left him panting and coated in sweat. After several minutes, however, he felt better, and he forced himself to look in her eyes. His breath caught at the emotion swimming in those beautiful blue depths. There was nothing guarded in her expression—even a blind man could have recognized that the tenderness in her gaze meant she cared for him. Deeply. His heart sank. Yes, cared deeply for a man whose true name and occupation she didn't even know. A man who'd lied to her. And who, he knew she would believe, had used her.

Damn.

His gaze shifted, his lips tightening at the sight of Waverly's body behind her. Then he glanced to her pelisse, the pale-gray wool ruined with his blood. The array of compresses stained with colors ranging from bright scarlet to barely pale pink. Finally he looked at where she held his hands, hers ungloved and stained with his blood. Would this be the last time he'd ever touch her?

He pulled in a breath, then raised his gaze to meet hers. "You admitted to me yesterday that you hadn't been entirely honest with me, that your circumstances weren't what you'd led me to believe. Now I must say the same thing to you. I don't work for a Mr. Jonas-Smythe. Indeed, there is no such person. I'm employed by the Crown."

Confusion passed over her features. "You're a steward for the Crown?"

"No. I gather information for them and assist in capturing individuals whose actions could threaten Britain."

She blinked. "You're a...*spy?*"

"Yes."

"A spy," she repeated in a bemused voice. "For how long?"

"Eight years."

"And how did you come to be a spy?"

"I volunteered." He hesitated, then continued, "My

family was wealthy and I'd never wanted for anything. Until eight years ago, I'd spent my life pursuing my own enjoyments, indulging my whims and desires, denied nothing. One night, while out carousing with a group of friends, we ventured into a pub, one in a less-fashionable part of London than we would normally visit. I struck up a conversation with the barkeep. His name was Billy. I asked him how he came to work at the bar—not because I was really interested, but because I thought his words might bring a laugh. Instead he...changed me."

He paused, shame filling him as it did every time he recalled the callow, selfish youth he'd been. "How?" she prompted.

"He told me about his life. He'd served in the navy and nearly died in battle. He'd survived, but lost a leg. When he came home, he needed work. Had a wife and son to look after. A friend of his owned the pub and he'd worked there ever since. Listening to him, hearing him talk of that battle, knowing it had to be painful for him to stand behind that bar for hours on end, that he did so out of love for his wife and child, gave me quite a jolt. It made me take a good at myself and my life. And I didn't like what I saw.

"I saw that while other men were serving our country, I'd simply moved from party to party, club to club, pleasure to pleasure, from one useless pursuit to the next. Frankly I was disgusted with myself. I wanted to change. To do something important. Something good. Something I could be proud of."

She nodded slowly. "I see. So...if we'd met eight years ago, I wouldn't have liked you."

"Most likely not. I don't see how you could have when I didn't like myself."

"And now? Do you like yourself now?"

"At this particular moment—not really. I lied to you. But in general…yes. I'm proud of the work I've done. The people I've helped. The lives I've protected and saved. Unfortunately with that sort of work comes secrecy, and with secrecy come lies. For eight years I've lied to my friends and my family—none of them know what I've just told you." He gave her hands a gentle squeeze. "I wouldn't have lied to you, Genevieve, if it hadn't been absolutely necessary."

She nodded slowly, clearly digesting his words. "All this means you didn't come to Little Longstone for a holiday while your employer was away on his wedding trip."

"No, I didn't." He took a bracing breath and forced himself to say the words he knew would drain the caring from her eyes. "I came to Little Longstone to find *you*. To retrieve the letter Lord Ridgemoor sent you for safekeeping."

All the color leaked from her face. He could almost hear the pieces clicking together in her mind. And then all the emotion faded from her eyes, until she stared at him as if she'd never seen him before. Even though he'd known it would happen, it still felt as if he'd been cut off at the knees. Without a word she slowly eased her hands from his. He wanted to snatch her hands back, to keep that connection, but he let her go. The loss made him feel as if his heart had been punctured.

"Tell me how you know about that," she said, her voice not quite steady.

And so he told her. All of it. Of Waverly's plot to kill Ridgemoor and frame Simon for the crime. Of Ridgemoor's last words. Of Simon confiding in Waverly and being granted the time to clear his name. Of renting the cottage. Repeatedly searching her home. Of her almost catching him that first time. She listened to all of it in complete silence, her gaze never moving from his, only growing bleaker until, when he finished, she simply stared at him with eyes that resembled two flat stones.

A full minute of the loudest silence he'd ever heard swelled between them. He wanted so badly to touch her, but he knew, *knew* she'd pull away from him. And he also knew that would break whatever small piece of his heart still remained intact.

"Richard is dead," she finally said in a voice as flat as her expression.

"Yes. I'm sorry. I know you cared for him."

"You knew all along that I wasn't a widow. That I'd been his mistress."

"Yes."

"You befriended me, flirted with me, spent time with me, *seduced* me—all to get the letter."

"No—"

She held up her hand to halt his words. The emptiness in her eyes was gone, replaced with a combination of pain, anger and betrayal that twisted his heart. "Do *not* lie to me again, Simon."

"I'm not lying. I admit that's why I came here and why I initially sought you out. But once I met you...you weren't what I expected. Genevieve, what we shared together, it's all been real."

Her eyes blazed at him and an incredulous sound escaped her. "Real? It's been based on nothing but lies! If you wanted the damn letter so badly, why didn't you simply ask me for it?"

He didn't immediately answer, and he saw the realization dawn in her widening eyes. "Dear God, you didn't ask me because you thought I might have been in some way connected to Richard's death."

"I couldn't ignore the possibility."

"So not only were you willing to seduce me for the letter, you did so believing I might have been either directly or indirectly responsible for my former lover's murder." The sound she made reverberated with disbelief. "These are actions you can be proud of?"

Without thinking, he reached for her hand. She jerked away as if he'd burned her, and his hand fell to his side. "I couldn't tell you the truth at first. All I knew of you was contained in the last desperate words of a dying man, words you cannot deny were more incriminating than exonerating. All I can tell you is that every moment I spent in your company served to convince me of your innocence."

"Yet still, you did not tell me the truth. Or ask me for the letter."

"I'd planned to do so as soon as I returned to the cottage this morning."

Another bitter sound. "Because you weren't able to find it after spending the night searching my home. And pawing through my personal belongings. Again."

He could think of ways to pretty up that bald statement, but what was the point? She was correct. "Yes." He cleared his throat. "As for seducing you…I want you to know that my mission and the letter were the last things on my mind when we were together. And that I…care for you."

The fire in her eyes extinguished like a snuffed-out candle. "'Care for me,'" she repeated in an utterly bleak tone. "Yes. That is obvious."

A sensation very close to panic gripped him. He had to make her understand. "Genevieve, I was trying to capture a murderer, a man, it turns out, who was a threat not only to me and you, but to England as well. I was going to tell you as soon as I could. I never meant to hurt you."

But he had. Hurt oozed from her like blood from a wound. And even if she forgave him, he knew she'd never forget. Or look at him with that same care he'd seen when he first opened his eyes. He tried to remind himself that in a mere few hours, as soon as he could travel, he'd be on his way to London. He'd never see her again. But instead of that reminder making him feel better, it only served to make his heart feel as if it had been ripped in two.

Her only reply was to rise, moving as if her limbs weighed an enormous amount. Then she turned her back to him and slowly headed toward the stairs.

"Where are you going?"

She paused, then glanced at him over her shoulder. "I'm going to get you your letter. After all, it's the reason you're here."

Simon watched her climb the stairs with labored steps. After she had disappeared from view, he struggled to his feet, resting his hand against the wall and closing his eyes to combat the waves of dizziness that hit him. When he opened his eyes he saw the folded piece of paper he'd offered to Waverly—the piece of paper that had saved him. Taking care not to keel over, he picked up the paper square and slipped it back into his pocket. By the time Genevieve rejoined him, he'd regained his equilibrium.

She stood in front of him, holding a gilt-edged frame. Her eyes remained expressionless, as if she'd pulled a curtain over her emotions. "Richard sent a note along with the box—a note I destroyed per his request—indicating he would come for it soon. Even though months had passed since we'd been together, the way he'd dismissed me still rankled, as did the fact that he took another mistress almost immediately, a very young, very beautiful woman. He didn't even have the decency to tell me face-to-face that he wished to end our arrangement. Instead he merely sent me a note."

Her lips pressed together briefly, then she continued, "I knew the box had to be of great importance and I was determined that he'd face me when he retrieved it. It took me hours to figure out the combination, but when I did, I discovered the letter inside. I suspected anywhere I tried to hide it would be discovered, just as I suspected Richard would try to retrieve the box and its contents without seeing me. I resolved to thwart him. Therefore, I hid the letter in plain sight by slipping it into an old picture frame and hanging it on my bedchamber wall, among all my other artwork and replicas of favorite poems." She held out the frame. "Here you are."

Simon took the frame and stared at the handwritten letter pressed beneath the glass and a swell of admiration hit him. "Very clever. I saw this hanging in your bedchamber—saw it, yet didn't really see it." He read the words, which appeared to be nothing more than a rather boring account of a day spent in the country, and his jaw tightened. "It's in code, as I suspected it would be. But according to Ridgemoor's last words, its message will prove Waverly's guilt and my innocence. Which means I owe you my life. For this and for tending to me after I was shot. Thank you, Genevieve."

A flicker of warmth broke through the blankness in

her eyes. "You're welcome. I...I hate that you lied to me, and I cannot deny I feel tricked. But since I've told many lies myself, I'm not precisely in a position to judge. I understand you only did what you believed you had to."

His gaze searched hers. "Do you? I hope so, because when we were together...you have my word I wasn't using you. You need to know that however this began, it changed course very quickly and became...something more."

"Yes, I suppose it did." Her gaze flicked to the frame. "I'm glad you have what you came for."

Encouraged by her words and that miniscule flash of warmth, he moved a step closer to her. His heart jumped with hope when she didn't back away. There was only one thing left to tell her, but surely if she could forgive him the other, larger transgressions, the fact that he'd omitted his title was a miniscule offense. "There's one more thing you should know about me, a very small thing, actually."

She appeared to brace herself. "What is it?"

"To protect my identity, I affected a slight change to my surname. It is actually Cooperstone."

She considered, then nodded. "Understandable, especially as there is a noble family that bears that same name."

"Yes, I know." He made her a formal bow. "Simon Cooperstone, Viscount Kilburn, at your service."

He wasn't certain what reaction he'd expected, but it certainly wasn't the dawning horror that bloomed on her face. The small amount of color she'd regained leeched from her cheeks, leaving her chalk-white. "You're a viscount." She said the word as if it harbored a contagious disease.

"Yes." Bloody hell, she looked as if she were going

to swoon. "Um, allowing for some understandable annoyance due to the deception, wouldn't most people think that's *good* news?"

"I'm afraid I'm not most people," she said in a barely audible voice.

Before he could say anything further, the door burst open. Baxter strode into the foyer, followed by a bespectacled man with gray hair carrying a black leather medical satchel, and a tall gentleman with an official air. Genevieve appeared to have gathered herself and performed the introductions. When she said his name and title, Baxter gaped at him.

"Viscount?" he repeated. "Yer a bloody *viscount?*"

Damn it, the man made it sound as if a *viscount* were synonymous with a *monster who eats children for breakfast.* "I'm afraid so."

The look Baxter shot him made it clear he'd like to murder him with his bare hands. Given the oppressive guilt weighing him down and the incessant pounding in his head, Simon wasn't entirely opposed to letting him, although he was at a loss to explain this unprecedented reaction to his title, which, even though he hadn't been honest about it, still seemed extreme.

He waded into the awkward silence and quickly told the magistrate what had occurred, giving him only the pertinent facts. After the magistrate and doctor verified that Waverly was, indeed, dead, Dr. Bailey asked Genevieve where he could examine Simon. She led them both to the sitting room while the magistrate, with Baxter's assistance, saw to the removal of Waverly's body.

Simon sat on the settee, his gaze fastened on Genevieve who stared out the window while Dr. Bailey examined his wound. He answered the doctor's questions by rote. No, he no longer felt nauseated or dizzy. Yes, his vision was fine. No, nothing other than his head hurt.

Well, that and his heart, which ached as if it had taken a lead ball dead center.

"How soon before I can travel?" Simon asked, wincing a bit as the doctor applied a salve to his wound.

"You were merely grazed, my lord—it bled a great deal as head wounds do, but except for the lump on your temple you escaped unscathed. Therefore, I'd say you can depart Little Longstone as soon as you like, although I'd recommend traveling by coach rather than on horseback."

"Is there a livery in town where I can secure a carriage?"

"Yes. I pass right by it on my way home. Would you like me to see to it for you?"

"Yes, thank you. I need to return to London as soon as possible."

Yes, he did. Which meant leaving Little Longstone... and Genevieve. Given the way she'd looked at him, she clearly wanted him gone. That was good. His life was in London. His job was in London. The sooner he left, the better.

His gaze remained on Genevieve, who continued to stare out the window while Dr. Bailey wrapped a linen bandage around his head. Bloody hell, she was so lovely. And she looked so lonely, standing there by herself. He ached to walk to her, take her in his arms. Would she allow him to? Based on her previous reaction, he doubted it. Indeed, she was more likely to whack him upside his head, which would completely finish him off. And if it didn't, Baxter would no doubt be delighted to do so.

He had to leave. She had to stay. He would never forget her, but their time together was over.

And surely, after the passage of some time, the raw edge of hurt sawing at him would fade away.

Surely it would.

GENEVIEVE stared out the sitting room as the words Simon had just spoken to Dr. Bailey echoed through her mind. *I need to return to London as soon as possible.* A humorless sound lodged in her throat. Actually, they weren't *Simon's* words—they were Viscount Kilburn's.

She squeezed her eyes shut. A viscount. Just another nasty jolt in a morning filled with them. First, thinking he would die. Then, realizing she loved him. Then, the muscle-loosening relief when he regained consciousness, followed by the foolish hope that maybe, somehow, they wouldn't have to say goodbye. That perhaps he'd come to care for her as she cared for him.

Finally, she'd listened to his admissions. All those lies. The heartbreak. The numbness. The disintegration of dreams she'd barely had time to acknowledge before they were snatched away. As much as she hated that he'd lied to her, she couldn't deny his reasons were valid. He didn't know her. Didn't know he could trust her. He'd done what was necessary to stop a killer—the man who'd murdered Richard—to save himself and other people.

The thought that he'd seduced her to gain access to her home, to the letter, filled her with a combination of hurt and fury that had made it hard to draw a breath. But his assurances that what may have started out that way had turned into something more…her heart had latched on to that, rekindling a spark of hope that his earlier words had extinguished.

So what had she done? Like a fool, she'd begun to hope again. Hope that they could, somehow, find a way to be together; build a life together. Her imagination had taken flight, weaving a happy ending that involved the two of them, standing before the vicar, taking vows to love and cherish. Genevieve Ralston, anonymous author, and Simon Cooper, operative for the Crown.

Except he wasn't Simon Cooper.

A huff of humorless air blew past her lips, fogging the window. A viscount. *Viscount.* That single word had popped the happy bubble she'd stupidly allowed to form in her mind. How had she made the same mistake again? How had she fallen in love with another man she couldn't have?

The sound of the door closing pulled her from her thoughts and she turned to discover she was alone with Simon. He rose from the settee and walked toward her. A snowy bandage encircled his head. An image of him on the floor, bleeding, flashed through her mind, and she blinked several times to dispel it.

He stopped when an arm's length separated them. "The doctor says I can travel. I'll be leaving for London as soon as my transportation is arranged."

"I understand." And she did. She just wished it didn't hurt so damnably bad.

"I have to go, Genevieve. It is my duty. I have to report to my superiors, give the letter to our decoders—"

"You don't have to explain any further, my lord. I know you have to go."

He frowned and moved closer, and it took all her strength not to back away, to stand her ground when all she wanted to do was run to her bedchamber, lock herself in and pretend that today had never happened. To pretend that he was a simple steward and she was just a woman in love.

But she stood her ground, even when he reached out and clasped her hands. His gaze searched hers and she forced herself not to look away. Why shouldn't she look her fill? It was the last time she would ever see him.

"It's Simon, not 'my lord,'" he said quietly. "I want you to know that this time I spent with you has been unforgettable."

She offered him a small smile. "I won't forget you, either…Simon." As much as she wished otherwise.

There was no missing the relief that filled his gaze, then his eyes turned serious. "Genevieve. I want to see you again. I don't want this to be goodbye."

Her stomach dropped to her toes with longing—and profound regret. She slipped her hands from his and shook her head. "I'm afraid this cannot be anything other than goodbye. I've been a nobleman's mistress, and it's an arrangement I've no desire to repeat." Indeed she'd vowed never to be another rich man's plaything, to be tossed aside when he tired of her. And given Simon's position in society, that's all she could ever be to him. "Continuing our physical relationship might satisfy us both for a short time, but let's not pretend it would last for long. My life is here, yours is in London and with your work. Eventually you'll need to marry and produce an heir, and I've no desire to share my lover with another woman, even if that woman is his wife. So I'm afraid that this has to be goodbye." She drew a deep breath and pressed on, praying her voice wouldn't break. "I'll always remember you fondly and hope you'll think of me the same way. I hope the rest of your life is wonderfully happy."

For several long seconds he said nothing, just looked at her with an unreadable expression. Finally he gave a nod. "Rest assured I shall always remember you fondly. And I hope the rest of your life is…magical." He reached for her hands and brought them to his mouth. "My darling Genevieve. Don't ever think you are anything less than perfect." His breath warmed her skin, as did the gentle kiss he pressed to the backs of her fingers. Without another word he released her, then turned and quit the room. The instant the door closed behind him, the tears she'd been fighting since she'd found him bleeding on her floor spilled from her eyes.

17

THE FIRST two weeks after Simon's departure passed in a slow parade of dreary days marked by crying jags and listless walks around the cottage. Genevieve now dreaded her daily jaunts to the springs—she couldn't erase from her mind the torturous image of her and Simon together. If the heated water wasn't necessary to relieve the pain in her hands, she'd never visit there again.

She tried to keep up her spirits in front of Baxter, but he wasn't fooled, and she knew he wanted, in his words, to "break that damn viscount into tiny pieces." She wished she could be angry with Simon, but she wasn't. He'd offered to continue their relationship. Indeed, he'd offered her the only thing he could. She was simply going to have to set her feelings aside, put them away using the same tactics she'd employed when Richard was no longer part of her life. The problem was, while she'd found a place inside her to submerge her feelings for Richard, there simply wasn't enough room for all the emotions, the wants and hopes and dreams Simon had inspired. Where could she possibly bury something so huge?

Fifteen days after Simon had left, a knock sounded on the door, and for several seconds Genevieve couldn't breathe as anticipation tore through her. Had he returned? Her ridiculous hope died when Baxter admitted an older gentleman who introduced himself as Mr. Lester Evans, a solicitor from London.

"I've a letter for you, Mrs. Ralston," Mr. Evans said, withdrawing an envelope from his waistcoat pocket. Genevieve froze at the sight of the maroon wax seal. It was Richard's crest. "I represented Lord Ridgemoor's interests for many years. He gave me this letter a year ago, instructing me to deliver it to you personally in the event of his death. I'm more sorry than I can say to be carrying out that wish. Should you have any questions or wish to contact me before I depart for London tomorrow morning, I'll be staying in the village, at the Sheepshead Inn."

Mystified, Genevieve watched him return to his elegant carriage, then she retired to her bedchamber. Sitting on the wing chair before the fire, she broke the wax seal and unfolded the single sheet of ivory vellum with hands that weren't quite steady.

My darling Genevieve,

Since the day I ended our arrangement, it has been my greatest hope to someday see you again, to stand in front of you and to give you these words in person. I'm sorry you're receiving them this way, through this letter. But under the circumstances, this unfortunately is the only way.

I've always prided myself on telling the truth, which made it so difficult to lie to you. And lie to you I did, when I told you I no longer wanted you. Genevieve, I've wanted you since the first moment I saw you, a beautiful young woman whose paintings touched my heart. I've loved you since the first time I touched you, a love I've never felt for another person. I know I hurt you when I ended our arrangement so abruptly and I can only say that doing so nearly killed me and filled me with a pain that has lived with me every moment since. But it had to be done. Threats had been made against me, and I realized that, given my feelings for you, you would be in danger. Certainly you would be the perfect weapon for my enemies to use against me—I'd give up anything for you, including my life, in a heartbeat, and I couldn't allow them to know that.

So I cut you from my life to guarantee your safety. I could stand being injured myself, but couldn't bear to think of any harm coming to you. Knowing your feelings for me, knowing the caring, loving woman you are, I had to push you away irrevocably, sever the tie between us completely, and that meant in a way that would hurt you, that would snuff out your feelings for me, that would prevent you from coming to me and that, thereby, would keep you safe. I want you to know it was the hardest thing I've ever done, and only the fact that the threats against me increased afterward enabled me to stay away from you, to not travel to Little Longstone, fall to my knees before you and beg your forgiveness. But you have to know that not a day, nay, not a moment passed that I didn't miss you, want you, love you with every breath.

While I can no longer ensure your physical well-being, I can guarantee your financial well-being. Toward that end, I have established an account in your name at the Bank of England, the details of which Mr. Evans, my solicitor, can help you with, along with giving you any other assistance you might require. I wish I could do more. And I wish I could be with you. Now. Always.

Thank you for loving me, darling Genevieve, and for allowing me to love you. You brought me nothing but joy. I hope you can forgive me. Please know that I wish you every happiness life can bring.

Yours,
Richard

GENEVIEVE stared down at words through eyes blurred with tears. He'd loved her. He'd always loved her. And he'd only wanted to keep her safe. A sense of relief—that she hadn't misjudged him, hadn't been the fool she'd believed herself to be for the past year—suffused her, mixing with grief for Richard's death, and sadness that he was irrevocably gone from her life, a brew of emotions that overwhelmed her. Setting the letter aside, she buried her face in her hands and cried. She wasn't certain how long she sat there, but when her tears finally ran out, the tightness and bitterness that had squeezed her heart for the past year was gone, replaced with a sense of peace and gratitude for having known and loved Richard. She'd let him go a year ago and although she'd been hurt, she'd moved on with her life—started again.

Fallen in love again.

With yet another man she couldn't have.

She could only pray her heart would heal a second time. But given the continued depth of her misery over the loss of Simon, she didn't think her prayers would be answered.

The next two weeks didn't pass any quicker than the

first two, nor were they any easier. Yet as the frequency of Baxter's pitying looks lessened, she assumed she became a better actress.

Exactly one month and two days after Simon had left, she decided she'd mourned long enough. The day dawned sunny and crisp, and she resolved this was the day she was going to smile again. Laugh again. And mean it. She'd start off with a long soak in the springs to loosen her sore joints, then spend some time writing. But first she'd reread all her pearls of wisdom to Today's Modern Woman. Hadn't she written that Today's Modern Woman didn't mope after a man? Yes, she had. And it was about time she took her own advice.

After a delicious breakfast of eggs, ham and Baxter's blueberry scones slathered with butter and jam, she bade her giant friend a cheery goodbye and headed toward the foyer.

"'Tis good to see ye smile, Gen," Baxter said. His own grin was tinged with such obvious relief she felt ashamed and annoyed at herself for not better hiding her misery from him.

"It feels good to do so. I'll be out for at least an hour. Why don't you walk to the village?" She adopted an innocent air as she donned her pelisse. "Isn't today the day Miss Winslow normally visits the butcher shop?"

A red flush crept all the way to the top of Baxter's bald head and he scowled. "Don't know. But seems we could use a bit o' bacon around here."

"Excellent idea." Satisfied that she'd done what she could to toss her friend in the path of the woman she hoped he'd soon realize he loved, she headed for the springs at a brisk pace. "Today I will be happy. Today I will be happy," she murmured. If she said it enough times, surely it would become fact. Indeed, she was smiling when she rounded the curve that brought her to the springs—a smile that froze along with her footsteps when she saw that her sanctuary was occupied.

Simon stood next to the bubbling water. Her stupefied gaze took in his dark-blue great coat, unfastened to reveal a jacket of the same color, a snowy white shirt and cravat, and buff breeches. His black boots gleamed, although the toe of the left one bore several unmistakable rows of teeth marks. In one hand he held Beauty's lead—no easy task as the dog had turned into a tail-wagging, tongue-lolling, barking bundle of canine energy that strained for freedom the instant she saw Genevieve. In Simon's other hand he held an enormous bouquet of pale-pink roses.

Their gazes met and every emotion, every feeling she'd struggled to bury for the past month ripped from its shallow grave to inundate her: the longing, the desire, the love. Before she could think of something to say, something that didn't include the phrases *I love you, I miss you, I'm miserable without you,* he let go of Beauty's lead.

The puppy raced toward her, and with a laugh Genevieve crouched down. Beauty greeted her with a plethora of wriggling doggie adoration. Genevieve ruffled her furry ears, scratched her scruff, then obediently rubbed Beauty's belly when the dog flopped on her back.

"She missed you."

Genevieve looked up. Simon stood less than six feet away, staring down at her with an indecipherable expression. After giving the dog another fond pat, she rose, refusing to acknowledge the unsteadiness in her knees. "I missed her, too. I cannot believe how much she's grown."

"Believe it. She eats me out of house and home. And unfortunately boots." He looked down at Beauty and said, "Heel." The dog immediately trotted to his side. "Sit." Beauty's rump instantly hit the ground. "Stay." He returned his attention to Genevieve. "*Stay* presents the biggest challenge, but she's getting better."

"I'm impressed. You've made a great deal of progress."

"Yes, although I think she only obeys me in those regards because she's so very bad when it comes to the boots." His gaze seemed to devour Genevieve, and it required all her fortitude to keep her expression bland. Even then, she wasn't certain she succeeded.

He cleared his throat and held out the flowers. "For you. I hope they're still your favorite."

She accepted the bouquet, ignoring the tingle that raced up her arms when her gloved fingers brushed his. "Yes, they are." She sank her face in the gorgeous blooms and took her time breathing in their heady fragrance in order to compose herself. "They're lovely. Thank you."

"You're welcome. They reminded me of you."

A long moment of silence swelled, one she waited for him to break. When it appeared he wasn't going to, she finally asked, "What are you doing here, Simon?"

"I wanted to speak with you and thought it best to do so here. I suspected that if I called at the cottage, my innards would be in Baxter's bare hands before I had the opportunity to open my mouth."

He was most likely correct. "What did you wish to speak to me about?"

"I thought you'd want to know that when the note Ridgemoor hid in the box was decoded, it named Waverly as the man who'd tried to kill him. It also provided irrefutable proof that Waverly was guilty of theft and treason."

"Was anyone else involved?"

"No. Waverly acted alone. Ridgemoor did England a great service by documenting Waverly's treachery in that letter. You should know that the earl died a hero."

Genevieve nodded slowly, then said, "Thank you for telling me, although it wasn't necessary for you to come all this way. You could have simply sent a note."

"No, as there's something I wish to give you. Return to you, actually, as it is yours." He reached in his pocket and withdrew a folded square of paper which he held out to her.

"What is that?" she asked, mystified, taking the proffered square.

"Unfold it."

She did so and stared at her own cramped handwriting. The smear of ink on the bottom. Her eyes passed over the words *Today's Modern Woman,* and a flush engulfed her entire body. She hadn't once considered that he would have found her writings in her desk, most likely because she hadn't had the heart to set pen to paper since he'd left.

"That piece of paper saved my life."

She pulled her gaze from the words to look at him. "I beg your pardon?"

"I found that in the wastebasket by your desk that last night I searched your cottage. I couldn't bring myself to let it be thrown away, so I folded it up and slipped it in my pocket. When Waverly demanded to know where the letter was, I claimed I had it and produced that. Dropping it on the floor between us offered me the split second of distraction I needed to dispatch him."

Genevieve swallowed. "I...I don't know what to say, other than that if it helped you in any way, I'm very glad you took it."

"As am I." His gaze probed hers, and she had the impression he could see directly into her soul. "You're Charles Brightmore."

She'd known what was coming, but hearing him say the words out loud still jolted her. "Would there be any point in denying it?"

The ghost of a smile whispered across his face. "No." He paused, then said, "You're immensely talented."

She hadn't expected that. "Th-thank you."

"And very insightful. I hope the second book is even more successful than the first one. You can be sure I'll be purchasing a copy."

"You're not...shocked?"

"No. I'm proud of you. And I wish you the very best in all your literary endeavors, especially this next one since, as I said, it saved my life. As for your Brightmore identity, you may rest assured your secret is safe with me."

She couldn't think of anything to say other than, "Thank you."

"My pleasure. Now, as to what I wanted to discuss with you—I've been thinking a great deal since I left Little Longstone, about many things. You, mostly. The time we spent together. And all those thoughts boiled down to one thing you said to me."

"And what was that?" she asked, trying not to sound as bemused as she felt.

"You said, 'I hope the rest of your life is wonderfully happy.'" His gaze searched hers. "Did you mean it?"

She nodded. "Yes, of course."

Something that looked like relief flashed in his eyes.

He smiled. "Excellent. I was hoping you'd say that. Well, I've decided that's what I hope for as well—for the rest of my life to be wonderfully happy. Once I concluded that, all I had to do was determine what would make it so. It didn't take me very long to figure that out. Indeed, it was very easy." He stepped toward her, and took her hand—the one that wasn't clutching the piece of paper and her flowers. "The answer is you, Genevieve. *You* are what I need to be wonderfully happy."

Genevieve went completely still. Then her heart, which had stuttered at his words, raced and tripped over itself. He wanted to continue their liaison. She'd vowed never to allow herself to be vulnerable again, never to risk her heart, never to be any man's mistress, but, dear God, she loved him. How could she even contemplate walking away from him now that he was here? Here, clearly wanting her to be his mistress. It was, of course, all a man in his position could offer her. She'd loved Richard and been his mistress, but Simon...she not only loved him, he owned her heart. How could she give him any less? For an answer, the vows she'd once made to herself crumbled like dust at her feet.

Before she could tell him, he said, "This last month has been the most miserable, lonely four weeks—plus two days—of my life and it is an experience I never want to repeat." He brushed his fingers over her cheek. "Dare I hope that you've been as miserable?"

She blinked. "You hope I've been unhappy?"

"It's been said that misery loves company, although *unhappy* is a lukewarm word for the way I hope you've felt." He moved a step closer. "I hope you've been utterly forlorn. Desolate. Despairing. Crushed. Joyless. Lonely. And excessively heartbroken." Another step closer. "Just as I have been."

Now less than two feet separated them, and she could see he looked drawn. As if he hadn't been eating or sleeping well. Her gaze flicked to his temple, but little evidence of his injury remained. "You've been all those things?"

A humorless sound huffed from between his lips. "Every single one. Since the moment I left your sitting room. And I don't want to feel them any longer. So— dare I hope you've been in the same pitiable state?"

"I cannot deny I've been sad, or that I've missed you."

"Excellent."

"Simon…about becoming your mistress—"

"I don't want you to be my mistress."

Confusion flooded her, which quickly turned to a hot wave of embarrassment at the realization he wasn't suggesting a liaison after all. "I'm sorry. I thought—"

"I want you to be my wife."

Genevieve could only stare. "Pardon?"

He cleared his throat, then said very slowly and distinctly, as if he were speaking to a small child, "I said, I want you to be my wife."

Dear God, his head injury had rattled his brain. "Simon, men in your position do not marry their mistresses." God knows she knew that well enough.

"The scandal could ruin you, ruin your family."

"Perhaps. But I can live with that. It's *you* I cannot live without. And you aren't my mistress."

"We slept together."

"Yes. And it is an event I want to repeat. Every night. For the rest of our lives." He cupped her face in his hands. "Genevieve. I haven't been the same since the first moment I saw you, when I hid behind the statue in your bedchamber. It was as if lightning stuck me. God knows I haven't been able to think of anything other than you. I knew I cared about you when I left Little Longstone, but I convinced myself I'd get over you. Forget my feelings." He gave a short laugh. "What a bloody nincompoop I was. I quickly learned the folly of *that* idiotic notion. I don't merely *care* for you. I am madly, insanely, arse-over-heels in love with you. I would have come sooner, but I wanted to settle my affairs so I wouldn't have to rush back to London."

Genevieve's heart was beating so wildly, he surely had to hear it. "You love me?"

"So much it hurts." He leaned forward and touched his forehead to hers. "So much I couldn't stand another day away from you. Not another hour. Not another minute."

"But your life is in London."

"That doesn't seem to matter—my heart is in Little Longstone."

Dear God, he sounded perfectly serious. "But what of your work for the Crown?"

He lifted his head and looked at her through green eyes that reflected the seriousness of his tone. "I am officially retired. As for my life in London, I'll keep my townhouse, but I've decided I'd rather spend the bulk of my time here. There is a fifty-acre tract of land for sale just west of the village. Beautiful trees, a lake, a pond and, best of all, four hot springs. It would be the perfect place to build a home."

She swallowed, trying to find her voice. "You're serious."

"Never more so. Before I came to Little Longstone, I'd been discontented. Something was missing from my life, but I didn't know what. Then I met you. One touch from you and I knew. *You* are what was missing. So now, the only questions are— Do you feel the same way I do?

Do you want the same things I do? And do you want to share your life with me?"

She actually felt the blood drain from her face. He meant it. Really, truly meant it. He loved her. Wanted to marry her. It was unbelievable. "My God," she whispered.

Alarm flickered in his eyes. "Bloody hell, you've gone pale. I don't think that's good."

A laugh escaped her, one that turned into a sob. His alarm grew. "Oh, God, you're crying. I *know* that's not good."

Another laugh and sob. "I'm not crying. I'm... stunned. And deliriously happy." She set down her flowers and paper then framed his face between her hands. "I feel exactly the same way you do—I love you so much I can barely *breathe*. And I want the same things you do—to build a beautiful home together in Little Longstone. And I want, more than anything, to share my life with you."

Anything else she might have said was lost when he snatched her against him and covered her mouth in a deep kiss filled with love and hope and passion. When he finally raised his head, he said, "I thought you were going to be stubborn and say no."

"And what would you have done if I had?"

"There are six dozen more roses in my carriage. Along with the finest art supplies I could find—in the hopes that they'd encourage you to paint something for me."

Emotion clogged her throat at the extravagant, romantic gesture. "That's...lovely. And so thoughtful. I'd like to do that. Very much."

"Excellent. But in case you still proved stubborn, there is also something else in the carriage—the Kilburn sapphire."

"The Kilburn sapphire?" she repeated weakly.

He nodded. "Ridiculously large at five carats, but in spite of its gaudiness, impressive just the same. The Kilburn diamond is a more manageable three carats, but as I recall you saying you found diamonds cold and lifeless, I thought the sapphire a better choice for an engagement ring."

A breathless laugh escaped her. "Really, all you needed to do was kiss me and tell me you loved me."

"Now you tell me," he teased. "I can see you're going to be easy to please."

"On the contrary, I'm going to be very demanding. Especially in the bedchamber, as all Today's Modern Women are."

"I don't know when I've heard better news." He peeled off her gloves and pressed a dozen kisses to her bare hands. "Please tell me you don't want a long engagement."

Heat and love and desire and pure, utter happiness whirled through her. "There are still two weeks left in November. How do you feel about a November wedding?"

His smile dazzled her. "My darling Genevieve, it just so happens that as with everything pertaining to you, I harbor a profound weakness for them."

* * * * *

*Celebrate 60 years of pure reading pleasure
with Harlequin®!*

To commemorate the event, Silhouette Special
Edition invites you to Ashley O'Ballivan's bed-
and-breakfast in the small town of Stone Creek.
The beautiful innkeeper will have her hands full
caring for her old flame Jack McCall. He's on the
run and recovering from a mysterious illness, but
that won't stop him from trying to win Ashley back.

*Enjoy an exclusive glimpse of Linda Lael Miller's
AT HOME IN STONE CREEK
Available in November 2009
from Silhouette Special Edition®*

The helicopter swung abruptly sideways in a dizzying arch, setting Jack McCall's fever-ravaged brain spinning.

His friend's voice sounded tinny, coming through the earphones. "You belong in a hospital," he said. "Not some backwater bed-and-breakfast."

All Jack really knew about the virus raging through his system was that it wasn't contagious, and there was no known treatment for it besides a lot of rest and quiet. "I don't like hospitals," he responded, hoping he sounded like his normal self. "They're full of sick people."

Vince Griffin chuckled but it was a dry sound, rough at the edges. "What's in Stone Creek, Arizona?" he asked. "Besides a whole lot of nothin'?"

Ashley O'Ballivan was in Stone Creek, and she was a whole lot of somethin', but Jack had neither the strength nor the inclination to explain. After the way he'd ducked out six months before, he didn't expect a welcome, knew he didn't deserve one. But Ashley, being Ashley, would take him in whatever her misgivings.

He had to get to Ashley; he'd be all right.

He closed his eyes, letting the fever swallow him.

There was no telling how much time had passed when he became aware of the chopper blades slowing overhead. Dimly, he saw the private ambulance waiting on the airfield outside of Stone Creek; it seemed that twilight had descended.

Jack sighed with relief. His clothes felt clammy against his flesh. His teeth began to chatter as two figures unloaded a gurney from the back of the ambulance and waited for the blades to stop.

"Great," Vince remarked, unsnapping his seat belt. "Those two look like volunteers, not real EMTs."

The chopper bounced sickeningly on its runners, and Vince, with a shake of his head, pushed open his door and jumped to the ground, head down.

Jack waited, wondering if he'd be able to stand on his own. After fumbling unsuccessfully with the buckle on his seat belt, he decided not.

When it was safe the EMTs approached, following Vince, who opened Jack's door.

His old friend Tanner Quinn stepped around Vince, his grin not quite reaching his eyes.

"You look like hell warmed over," he told Jack cheerfully.

"Since when are you an EMT?" Jack retorted.

Tanner reached in, wedged a shoulder under Jack's right arm and hauled him out of the chopper. His knees immediately buckled, and Vince stepped up, supporting him on the other side.

"In a place like Stone Creek," Tanner replied, "everybody helps out."

They reached the wheeled gurney, and Jack found himself on his back.

Tanner and the second man strapped him down, a process that brought back a few bad memories.

"Is there even a hospital in this place?" Vince asked irritably from somewhere in the night.

"There's a pretty good clinic over in Indian Rock," Tanner answered easily, "and it isn't far to Flagstaff." He paused to help his buddy hoist Jack and the gurney into the back of the ambulance. "You're in good hands, Jack. My wife is the best veterinarian in the state."

Jack laughed raggedly at that.

Vince muttered a curse.

Tanner climbed into the back beside him, perched on some kind of fold-down seat. The other man shut the doors.

"You in any pain?" Tanner said as his partner climbed into the driver's seat and started the engine.

"No." Jack looked up at his oldest and closest friend and wished he'd listened to Vince. Ever since he'd come down with the virus—a week after snatching a five-year-old girl back from her noncustodial parent, a small-time Colombian drug dealer—he hadn't been able to think about anyone or anything but Ashley. When he *could* think, anyway.

Now, in one of the first clearheaded moments he'd experienced since checking himself out of Bethesda the day before, he realized he might be making a major mistake. Not by facing Ashley—he owed her that much and a lot more. No, he could be putting her in danger, putting Tanner and his daughter and his pregnant wife in danger, too.

"I shouldn't have come here," he said, keeping his voice low.

Tanner shook his head, his jaw clamped down hard as though he was irritated by Jack's statement.

"This is where you belong," Tanner insisted. "If you'd had sense enough to know that six months ago, old buddy, when you bailed on Ashley without so much as a fare-thee-well, you wouldn't be in this mess."

Ashley. The name had run through his mind a million times in those six months, but hearing somebody say it out loud was like having a fist close around his insides and squeeze hard.

Jack couldn't speak.

Tanner didn't press for further conversation.

The ambulance bumped over country roads, finally hitting smooth blacktop.

"Here we are," Tanner said. "Ashley's place."

* * * * *

Will Jack be able to
patch things up with Ashley,
or will his past put the woman he loves
in harm's way?
Find out in
AT HOME IN STONE CREEK
by Linda Lael Miller
Available November 2009
from Silhouette Special Edition®

This November,
Silhouette Special Edition®
brings you

NEW YORK TIMES
BESTSELLING AUTHOR

LINDA LAEL
MILLER

At Home in
Stone Creek

Available in November
wherever books are sold.

SSELLM60BPA

Silhouette Desire

**FROM *NEW YORK TIMES*
BESTSELLING AUTHOR**

DIANA
PALMER

THE
MAVERICK

**A BRAND-NEW
LONG, TALL
TEXAN STORY**

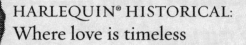

HARLEQUIN® HISTORICAL:
Where love is timeless

The Winter Queen
AMANDA MCCABE

Lady-in-waiting to Queen Elizabeth,
Lady Rosamund Ramsay lives at the heart
of glittering court life. Charming Dutch
merchant Anton Gustavson is a great favorite
among the English ladies—but only Rosamund
has captured his interest! Anton knows just
how to woo Rosamund, and it will be a
Christmas season she will never forget....

*Available November 2009
wherever books are sold.*

REQUEST YOUR FREE BOOKS!

2 FREE NOVELS
PLUS 2
FREE GIFTS!

HARLEQUIN®

Blaze

Red-hot reads!

YES! Please send me 2 FREE Harlequin® Blaze™ novels and my 2 FREE gifts (gifts are worth about $10). After receiving them, if I don't wish to receive any more books, I can return the shipping statement marked "cancel". If I don't cancel, I will receive 6 brand-new novels every month and be billed just $4.24 per book in the U.S. or $4.71 per book in Canada. That's a savings of 15% off the cover price. It's quite a bargain. Shipping and handling is just 50¢ per book.* I understand that accepting the 2 free books and gifts places me under no obligation to buy anything. I can always return a shipment and cancel at any time. Even if I never buy another book, the two free books and gifts are mine to keep forever.

151 HDN EYS2   351 HDN EYTE

Name	(PLEASE PRINT)	
Address		Apt. #
City	State/Prov.	Zip/Postal Code

Signature (if under 18, a parent or guardian must sign)

Mail to the **Harlequin Reader Service:**
IN U.S.A.: P.O. Box 1867, Buffalo, NY 14240-1867
IN CANADA: P.O. Box 609, Fort Erie, Ontario L2A 5X3

Not valid to current subscribers of Harlequin Blaze books.

Want to try two free books from another line?
Call 1-800-873-8635 or visit www.morefreebooks.com.

* Terms and prices subject to change without notice. Prices do not include applicable taxes. N.Y. residents add applicable sales tax. Canadian residents will be charged applicable provincial taxes and GST. Offer not valid in Quebec. This offer is limited to one order per household. All orders subject to approval. Credit or debit balances in a customer's account(s) may be offset by any other outstanding balance owed by or to the customer. Please allow 4 to 6 weeks for delivery. Offer available while quantities last.

Your Privacy: Harlequin Books is committed to protecting your privacy. Our Privacy Policy is available online at www.eHarlequin.com or upon request from the Reader Service. From time to time we make our lists of customers available to reputable third parties who may have a product or service of interest to you. If you would prefer we not share your name and address, please check here. ☐

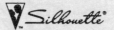

SPECIAL EDITION

FROM *NEW YORK TIMES* BESTSELLING AUTHOR

Ashley O'Ballivan had her heart broken by a man years
ago—and now he's mysteriously back. Jack McCall *isn't*
the person she thinks he is. For her sake, he must keep
his distance, but his feelings for her are powerful.
To protect her—from his enemies and himself—he
has to leave…vowing to fight his way home to
her and Stone Creek forever.

Available in November wherever books are sold.

Visit Silhouette Books at www.eHarlequin.com

HARLEQUIN *Blaze*

COMING NEXT MONTH
Available October 27, 2009

#501 MORE BLAZING BEDTIME STORIES Julie Leto and Leslie Kelly
Encounters
Fairy tales have never been so hot! Let bestselling authors Julie Leto and
Leslie Kelly tell you a bedtime story that will inspire you to do anything but sleep!

#502 POWER PLAY Nancy Warren
Forbidden Fantasies
Forced to share a hotel room one night with a sexy hockey-playing cop,
Emily Saunders must keep her hands to herself. Not easy for a massage
therapist who's just *itching* to touch Jonah Betts's gorgeous muscles. But all
bets are off when he suddenly makes a play for her!

#503 HOT SPELL Michelle Rowen
The Wrong Bed
As a modern-day ghost buster, Amanda LeGrange is used to dealing with the
unexplained. But when an ancient spell causes her to fall into bed with her sexy
enemy, she's definitely flustered. Especially since he's made it clear he likes her
hands on him when they're out of bed, as well....

#504 HOLD ON TO THE NIGHTS Karen Foley
Dressed to Thrill
Hollywood's hottest heartthrob, Graeme Hamilton, is often called the world's
sexiest bachelor. Only Lara Whitfield knows the truth. Sure, Graeme's sexy
enough.... But he's very much married—to her!

#505 *SEALED* AND DELIVERED Jill Monroe
Uniformly Hot!
Great bod—check. Firm, kissable lips—check. Military man—check.
Hailey Sutherland has found *the* guy to share some sexy moments with. In
charge of SEAL training, Nate Peterson's not shocked by much, but he is by
Hailey's attitude. He just hopes the gorgeous woman can handle as much
attitude in the bedroom....

#506 ZERO CONTROL Lori Wilde
Though Roxanne Stanley put the *girl* in girl-next-door, she *wants*
Dougal Lockhart. Now! What she doesn't know: the hottie security expert is
undercover at the sensual fantasy resort to expose a criminal, but it may be her
own secret that gets exposed....

HBCNMBPA1009